"You really don't w... get involved with me, Bart Collingsworth. You really don't want to get involved with me."

He touched her arm. "Why don't you let me be the judge of that?"

Jaclyn didn't answer, but when he took her hand in his, she let him lead her back to the porch. "Tell me one good reason I should trust you."

Bart smiled. "Because from the looks of things, you don't have anyone else to go to for help and I'm offering."

"You're making a big mistake, cowboy. A monumental mistake."

JOANNA WAYNE

TEXAS GUN SMOKE

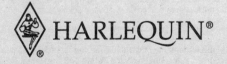

HARLEQUIN®

TORONTO • NEW YORK • LONDON
AMSTERDAM • PARIS • SYDNEY • HAMBURG
STOCKHOLM • ATHENS • TOKYO • MILAN • MADRID
PRAGUE • WARSAW • BUDAPEST • AUCKLAND

Thanks to all the readers out there who love a good romance and keep buying my books. A special thanks goes to Ruth Foreman, a reader who has been with me since my very first book. Though we've never met in person, we have become good friends via e-mail. She is a constant source of inspiration, an optimistic, cheerful person dedicated to her faith and family. Even losing her home to the devastating floods of Katrina couldn't destroy her loving spirit. She's the kind of fan that makes writing a real joy.

ISBN-13: 978-0-373-88793-4
ISBN-10: 0-373-88793-0

TEXAS GUN SMOKE

ABOUT THE AUTHOR

Joanna Wayne was born and raised in Shreveport, Louisiana, and received her undergraduate and graduate degrees from LSU-Shreveport. She moved to New Orleans in 1984, and it was there that she attended her first writing class and joined her first professional writing organization. Her first novel, *Deep in the Bayou*, was published in 1994.

Now, dozens of published books later, Joanna has made a name for herself as being on the cutting edge of romantic suspense in both series and single-title novels. She has been on the Waldenbooks Bestselling List for romance and has won many industry awards. She is a popular speaker at writing organizations and local community functions and has taught creative writing at the University of New Orleans Metropolitan College.

She currently resides in a small community forty miles north of Houston, Texas, with her husband. Though she still has many family and emotional ties to Louisiana, she loves living in the Lone Star state. You may write Joanna at: P.O. Box 265, Montgomery, TX 77356.

Books by Joanna Wayne

CAST OF CHARACTERS

Bart Collingsworth—Convinced Jaclyn is in trouble, he feels compelled to help her and must fight the almost overwhelming attraction he feels from the moment they meet.

Jaclyn McGregor—Though wary, she is forced to accept Bart Collingsworth's help in finding her friend, who has disappeared without a trace.

Lenora Collingsworth—The strong but loving matriarch of the Collingsworth clan.

Langston, Matt and Zach Collingsworth—Bart's brothers.

Jaime Collingsworth and Becky Ridgely—Bart's sisters, both of whom live at Jack's Bluff Ranch.

Margo Kite—Jaclyn's friend who has disappeared from New Orleans.

Ed Guerra—Local Texas sheriff.

Senator Patrick Hebert—Louisiana politician believed to have been having an affair with Margo Kite before her disappearance.

Candy Hebert—The senator's wife.

Win Bronson—Senator Hebert's right-hand man.

Rene Clark—Foreman at Paradise Pleasures, a small Texas ranch owned by the senator and some of his friends.

Clay Markham—Private investigator hired by Bart Collingsworth.

Chapter One

A light rain started to fall, making the road that wound its way to Jack's Bluff Ranch dangerously slick. Not a safe night out for man nor beast. Most days Bart fell into the former category. He slowed his pickup truck and turned up the volume on his radio, singing along with George Strait, though one of them was a bit off-key.

Bart stretched, then shed the necktie he'd loosened much earlier. He hadn't wanted to drive into Houston tonight, especially in this monkey suit. But his mother had refused to take no for an answer. Not that he didn't agree with her that philanthropy was important or that her work in spearheading the drive to raise funding for the new children's wing at the hospital was a worthy task; but sipping champagne and making small talk with a gaggle of rich socialites wasn't his scene.

It still amazed him that his mother could waltz from ranch life at Jack's Bluff to Houston society functions so effortlessly. The only dance Bart knew was the two-step, and that was the way he liked it.

His mom had opted to stay in town and spend the night with his brother Langston and his new family, leaving Bart to make the hour-plus drive home alone. Normally he wouldn't have minded, but tonight he could have used the company just to stay awake and alert. It had been a long day. Ranching was not a nine-to-five job.

He caught sight of a pair of bucks at the edge of the road in front of him. He slowed even more. You never knew when a deer would take a notion to run right in front of you. He'd totaled a pickup like that last year. Worse part was it had killed the doe.

The rain picked up. He turned on the defroster to clear the windshield. The visibility improved only slightly, but he'd be home in less than ten minutes.

He tried to stifle a yawn, then jerked to attention. What the hell? Two cars were speeding toward him, driving so close they were all but swapping paint.

A second later he saw sparks fly as the outside car sideswiped the other and sent it rocking and bouncing along the shoulder before the driver managed to get all four wheels back on the highway. If this was some teenage game of chicken, they were taking things way too far. Somebody was likely to get killed. Maybe him.

He slowed and took the shoulder as the cars collided again. This time the smaller one went flying off the road. It slid down an incline and then rolled over, coming to a rocking upside-down stop a few yards ahead of Bart. The lunatic driving the attacking car sped past him.

Bart screeched to a stop, grabbed a flashlight and jumped from his truck. He took off running toward the wrecked car. Its wheels were still spinning when he got to it.

He aimed a beam of illumination inside the car. There was only one occupant—a woman who was draped over the steering wheel, upside down but still held in place by her seat belt. Blood trickled across her left temple and matted in her blond hair. She lifted her head, shaded her eyes from the light and shrank away from him.

The door was jammed, and he had to work with it for a few seconds to pry it open. "Are you okay?"

She didn't answer, but her face was a pasty white and her eyes were wide with fear.

"Take it easy. You're safe now."

"You tried to kill me."

"Not me, but someone did." He leaned in closer so that he could see the head wound. The cut didn't look particularly deep, but a nice little goose egg was forming. "What hurts?"

She stared at him, looking dazed and still fearful as she touched her fingertips to the blood. "I must have hit my head."

"Probably against the side window when you went into the roll. For some reason, your air bag didn't deploy."

"The light had gone off. I was going to get it checked."

A little late for that now. He pulled her against him while he loosened the seat belt.

He lifted her out of the car and stood her on the ground. She was lighter than a newborn calf and short, probably no more than five-two or -three. Thin, almost waiflike. But movie-star pretty.

She swayed, and he put an arm around her shoulder for support. "My truck's over there." He pointed to where it was parked on the opposite side of the road. "Let's get you in it and out of the rain while we wait for an ambulance."

"No!" Fear pummeled her voice. "No ambulance. I'll be okay. I just…" She swayed again and might have lost her balance completely if he hadn't been supporting her. "I just need a minute for my head to clear. And I need my handbag."

"Right." He found it with its strap tangled in the brake and accelerator pedals. He worked it loose and handed it to her. She clasped it tightly in both hands as rain dripped from her hair and rolled down her face. He pulled the silk handkerchief from his breast pocket and wiped the water and blood away.

"Who are you?" she whispered, her voice shaky.

"Bart Collingsworth. And don't worry. I'm just a Good Samaritan who happened to be passing by."

He took her hand and led her across the street. Once she was safely settled in the passenger seat, he closed the door, calling 911 as he rounded the truck to the driver's side. Like it or not, he was calling for an ambulance and law enforcement. He was still giving the operator the information when he climbed behind the wheel.

"I know you said you don't want an ambulance," he said once he'd broken the connection. "But there's a small hospital in Colts Run Cross—not much more than a clinic with a few beds, but they'll call in a doctor to check you out. Better to be safe than sorry."

"I've already had more than enough of Colts Run Cross."

"I take it you're not from around here."

She stared out the front window into the darkness and rain. "Is anybody?"

"A few lucky souls. I live on a ranch a few miles down the road. Jack's Bluff. You just passed it."

She trembled and clasped her hands in

front of her, nervously twisting the wedding band on her left hand. "I didn't notice."

"Guess not, with that lunatic trying to run you off the road. What was that about?"

"I haven't a clue."

"Then you don't know the driver of the other car?"

"No."

"But you must have had some kind of altercation for him to react so violently."

"He just came out of nowhere, sped up behind me and forced me off the road."

Either she was lying or this made no sense at all.

She leaned back and closed her eyes. She looked incredibly fragile, like a porcelain doll that had been left out in the rain.

"Are you sure you're okay?"

"I'm fine. I just don't feel like talking."

He left it at that until she finally shifted and opened her eyes, still looking straight ahead.

"You know, if you really want to be a Good Samaritan," she said, "you could drive me into town and drop me off at a cheap motel. I can handle things from there."

"You were awful woozy back there. You'd

be better off seeing a doctor. But you're welcome to use my phone if you want to call your husband."

She twisted the gold band on her finger as she shook her head. "No, thanks."

"I can call for someone to tow your car or you can just wait and have the sheriff do it."

Finally she turned to face him. "If you live on a ranch, why are you dressed like that?"

"It was tux night at the campfire. But I'm a genuine cowboy. Got boots and spurs and everything."

"Then maybe you could get some of your cowboy buddies to pull my car back to Jack's whatever you said."

"Jack's Bluff."

"Right. Take the car there and I'll come for it later."

"Your car's got four wheels straight up in the air. You need a tow truck for this job."

She shrugged. "I'm short of cash and I don't have a credit card on me."

"Tell you what—I know a local mechanic with his own tow truck. I'll call Hank Tanner and have him take the car to his garage. You can settle up with him later."

"Whatever."

"He'll want a name."

"Jaclyn."

Sirens sounded, and Bart caught sight of flashing lights speeding toward them. The ambulance had made excellent time.

"Last name?" he asked.

She ignored the question.

"If you're in some kind of trouble, you should level with me. Maybe I can help. I could at least follow the ambulance to the hospital and see that you're in good hands tonight."

"In trouble? I *am* trouble, cowboy. Thanks for the offer. But forget about the car. Forget about me, too. I'll be just fine." In spite of her assurances, a tear escaped and rolled down her right cheek.

Bart's insides kicked around like a stallion on a short rope. He had his doubts that anything she'd said tonight had been the truth. Well, except that she was trouble. Likely in trouble, as well. None of which was any of his business.

But he was wide-awake now, and the hospital wasn't but a few miles away. Besides, what red-blooded cowboy could resist trouble that came in a package that was five foot two and blond?

Chapter Two

Sheriff Ed Guerra had called just as Bart was about to follow the ambulance into town. Once Bart gave him the lowdown, the sheriff asked Bart to hang around. Bart couldn't think of a good reason to refuse.

There was no trace of the sheriff's usual good humor when he strode over to the crime scene in the steady rain. Bart had already dug his work poncho from the metal toolbox in the bed of his truck, along with an old Western hat that had seen better days. The temperature was supposed to turn a bit cooler following the front that produced the rain, but right now it was still warm and muggy for late October.

Ed adjusted his umbrella as he approached the upside-down car. "Well, don't this just take the whole biscuit! You can bet there's a dadgum sight more to this story than meets the eye."

"I took the liberty of checking in the glove compartment for the registration papers on the car. The vehicle belongs to Margo Kite of New Orleans, Louisiana," Bart said, handing the document to the sheriff.

Ed held it under the umbrella so it wouldn't get wet while he adjusted his flashlight to illuminate it. "But you said the driver's name was Jackie."

"Jaclyn—at least that's what she told me, but she could have been lying. She wouldn't give a last name. I guess the car could have been borrowed."

"Or stolen," Ed said. "Approximate age of the injured?"

"Early twenties."

Ed rubbed his chin. "Not a teenager, then. Was she under the influence?"

"I didn't smell alcohol on her breath."

"Stoned?"

"Didn't appear to be."

"Pretty?"

"Not bad."

"I was afraid of that. The pretty ones are always the most trouble."

"I'll add that to my list of truths to live by."

"No, you won't. You young studs never do. I'll run a check on the license plate. See what turns up."

Bart took a better look at the car while the sheriff made his call. It was a late-model Buick Lacrosse in an off-red metallic finish. It would take a skilled body man to put it back in decent shape.

Only the trunk seemed to be relatively undamaged. Bart opened it and pulled out a blue nylon duffel with a slight rip in the side, apparently not as important to Jaclyn as her handbag had been. The only other items in the trunk were the typical spare tire, a few tools and three liter-size diet sodas that would probably spew their contents the second they were opened.

"Car hasn't been reported as stolen," the sheriff said as he rejoined a Bart a few minutes later. "Your Jaclyn might have borrowed it from New Orleans Margo."

"She's not *my* Jaclyn, but she did say she was from out of town."

"Did you get a good look at the car that ran this one off the road?"

"I saw two bright lights coming at me and then a blur of metal as it sped past. New-style headlights, so I'd say it was a late-model car. A full-size sedan, but I can't give you the make, color or any identifying marks—except that it had to take some serious damage when it collided with the Buick."

"I'll have all the area body shops keep a look out for it, but unless the driver's got peanuts for brains, he won't take it anywhere near here to have it repaired. And he won't be driving around Colts Run Cross with the telltale damage."

"My guess is he's not from around here," Bart said. "The locals aren't given to road rage."

"I'd have to agree," Ed said. "More likely this is trouble Jaclyn brought with her from Louisiana. Did she say why she was in the area?"

"No, actually, she said very little. She was woozy at first and then clammed up except for saying that she didn't need an ambulance."

"But she left in an ambulance, right?"

Bart nodded. "They were taking her to the hospital in Colts Run Cross."

"Good. I'll question her there. You say you don't think she was seriously injured."

"She had a blossoming goose egg on the left side of her head next to a wound that oozed blood, but she didn't appear to have any broken bones or to be in much pain."

Ed looked back to the car and shook his head. "She's lucky to walk away from that."

"Damn lucky."

"Okeydoke. I'm going to call Hank's Garage and tell him this is a two-man towing job. Then I'll shoot some pictures of the car while I'm waiting on Hank. That camera of mine don't take the sharpest of photos in the dark, but it will have to do. If I wait until morning and this happens to go to trial, some slick city lawyer will say the crime scene was compromised overnight. Humph. Compromised by a bunch of field mice and armadillos."

"I have Mother's fancy camera in my truck. She wanted pictures of the reception tonight."

"Reception, huh? That explains why you're

wading mud in those city-slicker shoes. They're ruined now anyway, so how about you taking over as crime-scene photographer?"

"I can handle it." Bart went to his truck for the camera. The duffel was still in his hand, so he tossed that into the backseat of the extended cab. That gave him an even better reason to show up at the hospital. Not that the sheriff couldn't have taken it with him.

When Bart returned, Ed was on the phone with Hank and aiming his superbright flashlight at the skid marks in the middle of the road.

"Definitely looks intentional," Ed said when he'd finished with Hank. "Little Miss Jaclyn has some tough enemies or some real mean friends."

"Looks that way. But she isn't a 'miss.' She was wearing a wedding band."

"Bingo. When there's a husband or a boyfriend, I always have a first lead."

Anger surged inside Bart as he snapped pictures, first of the skid marks and then walking around the car to get views from every angle. He hoped Ed was wrong about the husband being behind this. It was tough to think any man could do this to a woman. But a man who'd sworn to love and cherish Jaclyn…what kind of perverted bastard would he have to be to pull a stunt like this?

"That should do it," Ed said after Bart had taken a couple dozen shots. "As soon as Hank gets this vehicle righted and on the tow truck, I'm going to the hospital and have a talk with the victim. I'll keep you posted as to how this turns out."

Bart nodded and said his goodbyes without mentioning that he planned to stop by the hospital as well. He didn't want to have to explain his reason for doing so, mainly because he didn't really understand it himself.

He climbed behind the wheel, turned the key in the ignition and pulled onto the highway. Five minutes later he reached the gate to Jack's Bluff. He could turn in and forget all about no-last-name Jaclyn just as she'd told him to do. But whatever she was into, whether her husband was behind her trouble or not, she definitely could use a friend with a broad shoulder to lean on tonight.

His shoulders had nothing better to do.

BART HAD BEEN AT THE hospital for over an hour before Dr. Cane—a tall, lanky fellow with unruly shocks of bright red hair and horn-rimmed glasses—finally came to the emergency waiting room to give him an update. "The patient is seriously disoriented and experiencing traumatic amnesia, probably caused by swelling near the brain."

Bart stared at Dr. Cane. "Are we talking about the same woman? The one involved in the car wreck less than two hours ago?"

"That's the one. The ambulance driver said you gave her name as Jaclyn, but she's not responding to that now. She has no knowledge of who she is or how she got here."

"Did you look in her handbag for identification?"

"Two of the nurses searched the purse and wallet thoroughly. There was no driver's license or any other form of identification." Dr. Cane scratched his whiskered chin. "How did she seem when you were with her?"

"She was a tad woozy when I pulled her out of the car," Bart admitted, "but she was responsive. We carried on a conversation of sorts."

"That would be consistent with the diagnosis of transient amnesia due to trauma. The increased swelling from the time of the wreck until the present has interfered with memory functions. This is unusual but not unheard of, even with a minor concussion such as the patient has."

"How long do you expect the amnesia to continue?"

"Just until the swelling is reduced. She could be functioning normally in a few hours or it could last as long as a couple of days. It would be extremely rare for it to continue for more than forty-eight hours but not impossible."

There was no reason not to believe Dr. Cane's diagnosis, but still Bart had a hard time buying it. "Do you think she could be faking the amnesia?"

"That's always a possibility."

And with Jaclyn, Bart considered it more than a possibility. There were just too many things that didn't add up, like what a Louisiana girl was doing on a dark Texas road alone so late at night. And more bizarre, why had some homicidal crackpot decided to run her off the road for no apparent reason?

Dr. Cane pushed his glasses up the bridge

of his nose. "We're keeping her overnight for observation, longer if necessary. I'll consult with a neurologist tomorrow, but if her condition worsens or continues past forty-eight hours, we'll move her to a facility in Houston."

"Can I see the patient?"

"I don't see why not. Since you're the last one she spoke to before the onset of amnesia symptoms, seeing you might trigger a memory. But don't tire her out or upset her. The sheriff called and he's on his way to the hospital to question her about the wreck. He was just waiting for us to finish the examination and assign her to a room. She's in 224."

Bart thanked the doctor for the info and took the stairs to the second floor.

"What brings you out on such a rainy night?"

He stared at the nurse who'd spoken, a girl he'd graduated with from Colts Run Cross High School. No longer a girl, she was pregnant—and from the looks of the bulge, ready to deliver most any day.

"Hi, Cindy. I didn't know you were working here."

"Yeah, for just over a year. I worked in Houston for a while, but when I got married we decided to move back here. I married Bud Johnson. You remember him. He was a couple of years ahead of us."

"I remember." And he really didn't want to make small talk tonight. "I'm here to see the patient who was admitted tonight with a concussion."

"Oh, the mystery woman. How do you know her?"

"I don't. I just came up on the car wreck after it happened."

"Then you must be the one who called for the ambulance. She doesn't remember any of that."

"So I heard." Bart held up the duffel. "I got this from her car and thought she might need it."

"Did you check it for ID?"

"No." He hadn't realized he'd need to until a few minutes ago.

"You can let her check it. She's awake. Room 224. But if the two of you find out who she is, we could sure use that information for her records."

"You got it." He stopped at the door and tapped lightly.

The whispered, "Come in," was so faint he could barely make it out.

He stepped inside. Jaclyn's light blue hospital gown fell off one slender shoulder as she rose to her elbows. She jerked it back in place, then stared at him blankly, either not recognizing him or doing a good job of faking it.

"Hello, Jaclyn. I brought you this," he said, swinging the duffel onto the foot of the bed. "It was in the trunk of your car. I thought you might need it."

"Who are you?"

"Name's Bart Collingsworth, but we've met before. I pulled you from the overturned vehicle earlier tonight."

"Then I should thank you, though I don't remember it. I don't even remember my name, but Dr. Cane says the fog will clear up quickly."

"Do you want me to go through your duffel and see if there's any identification in there?"

She stiffened and then shrank back into the blue gown that fit like a loose sheet. "If you'll hand it to me, I can do that for myself."

He handed it to her—and was exceedingly glad he had when she pulled out a pair of white lacy panties and a matching bra. She tossed them onto the bed without notice, working her way through a pair of jeans and two long-sleeved cotton shirts.

"There's nothing here that helps," she said.

"Someone ran you off the road. Does that help?"

"I'm afraid not."

"What about the name Margo Kite?"

"No."

She answered quickly, but not before he noted an impulsive wince. "If you're afraid of someone, Jaclyn, the sheriff can make sure you're protected."

"I'm not afraid."

He wasn't convinced. In fact, he was almost certain it was fear or apprehension that shadowed her slate-colored eyes. "Do you want me to stay with you until morning?"

"No. Why would I? I don't know you."

"Just an offer. I'll get out of here and let you rest, but if you change your mind about wanting company or if you need anything, you can have the pregnant nurse named Cindy give me a call. She knows how to get in touch with me."

But Jaclyn had turned away and was staring at the wall. He backed out of the room and quietly closed the door behind him. He still wasn't convinced she had transient or any other kind of amnesia, but whatever she was into, she didn't want his help. That was good enough reason to get the devil out of here and get some sleep himself. He had a busy day tomorrow. Still, his heart twisted a little when he looked back and saw how lost she looked in the formless hospital gown.

The pretty ones are the most trouble. Definitely a truism worth remembering.

JACLYN HEARD THE DOOR shut behind Bart and fought the unexpected but excruciating ache to call out to the cowboy with the quick humor and mesmerizing smile. She wouldn't let herself make that mistake, not when she knew his offer of help would be about as lasting as this little show she was putting on. As soon as he found out who she really was he wouldn't be able to get away from her fast enough.

He'd know already—they all would—if she hadn't gotten to her driver's license first. She'd taken it out of her handbag while she'd been waiting to see the doctor and hidden it beneath the folds of the bloodstained blouse she'd been wearing at the wreck.

So the hero cowboy could just go back to his bunkhouse and forget all about her.

Still, Bart Collingsworth had a way about him. Too bad that trusting anyone at this point could be a deadly mistake.

Chapter Three

Bart spent a restless night and got up aggravated with himself for letting thoughts of Jaclyn rob him of needed sleep. He had plenty to do without worrying about a woman who didn't want his help. He tried to concentrate on issues at hand, checking the progress of the new fence going up in the northwest pasture and meeting with his brother Matt to discuss the possibility of increasing their Angus herd size by ten percent over the next twelve months.

By noon the meeting with Matt had concluded and Jaclyn had moved to front and center of his thoughts again. He started to go up to the big house for lunch but instead drove right by it and toward the gate. It wouldn't hurt to check on her and make

certain she was recovering from amnesia—
if she'd ever actually had any memory
problems.

He reached the hospital at ten after twelve
and went straight to the second floor. A
middle-aged nurse carrying a meal tray
spotted him before he reached Jaclyn's room.

"You're one of Lenora Collingsworth's
sons, aren't you?"

"Yes, ma'am. I'm Bart." It was difficult to
go anywhere in Colts Run Cross and not run
into someone who knew him or a member of
his family.

"I'm Bev Garland. I know your mother
from our Feed the Children program. She's
on our board of directors."

"I'll tell her I ran into you."

"You must be here to see the mystery
woman."

"How did you guess?"

"Easy—she's our only patient. And I heard
you were the one who rescued her from the
wrecked car last night."

"I just happened to be the first one to show
up. How is she?"

"She ate a big breakfast and she seems to

be feeling fine, but she can't remember a thing. Poor woman. She can't even call her husband and tell him she's safe."

"Is it okay if I stop in and see her? I promise I won't stay long."

"Stay as long as you like, but I don't know how much conversation you'll get out of her. She hasn't said but a few words to any of us all morning. I think the confusion is making her depressed. I was just taking her a lunch tray. You can tag along with me."

"Thanks." His boots clomped across the tile while her rubber-sole shoes barely made a sound. The nurse balanced a tray of fried chicken, mashed potatoes and green peas in one hand and tapped on the door with the other, though she didn't wait for a response before pushing into Jaclyn's room.

"I have lunch and a visitor," the nurse announced in a singsong voice that sounded as though she was talking to a toddler.

She set the tray on the table that swung over the bed. The covers were tousled and pushed back. Jaclyn was nowhere in sight. "You have company, honey," the nurse said again, this time looking toward the closed bathroom door.

There was no response.

Bev asked about Bart's grandfather Jeremiah, who was recovering at home from a stroke, and listened to his explanation before walking to the bathroom door and tapping lightly.

Still no response. She knocked again, then turned the handle and pushed the door open. "Not in there," she said, turning back to Bart. She shrugged her shoulders and placed her hands on her bulging hips. "Now where did that woman get off to?"

"Are you certain she wasn't discharged?"

"I was standing right here when Dr. Cane said he wanted to keep her another day. The patient didn't even put up an argument." Bev opened the small locker built into the wall. "Now this is strange. Her clothes are missing."

"Looks as if she discharged herself," Bart said.

"I don't know where she'd go when she didn't even know her name."

Which gave a lot of credence to his belief that the amnesia was faked in the first place.

"I better call Dr. Cane and let him know

his patient ran out on him and her bill." The nurse was muttering to herself as she shuffled from the room.

Bart grabbed a piece of chicken on his way out. Seemed a sin to let good fried chicken go to waste. He took the stairs again and exited through the back door. He was almost to his truck when he caught a glimpse of someone hunched down and darting between cars.

A second glance and he knew it was Jaclyn, her handbag and duffel flung over her shoulder, trying car doors. He dashed across the parking lot, reaching her just as she found the kind of easy mark she'd been looking for. Not only was the door of the white compact car unlocked but the keys were also dangling from the ignition—not all that uncommon in Colts Run Cross.

Bart grabbed her arm as she started to climb behind the wheel. "Care to explain what you're doing?"

She groaned. "Don't you have a life?"

"Not nearly as exciting as yours."

"I was only going to borrow the car."

"We call taking a car without permission 'stealing' in Texas."

"You do have the quaintest customs." She stepped away from the car. "Now I suppose you're going to call that nice sheriff so that I can spend some time in one of your friendly jail cells."

"I'm giving it serious thought."

"Look, no harm was done. I didn't even start the engine. Why don't you forget the sheriff and give me a ride to the nearest Greyhound bus station so that I can go home?"

"What about your amnesia?"

"That's the neat thing, see. My memory came back, just like the doctor said it would."

"Then I guess you have a last name now?"

"Sure. It's Jones. Now are you going to give me a ride or not?"

Jaclyn Jones. He doubted that. "Why take a bus? You could just rent another car. The one you were in is going to be out of commission for a while."

"Like I said last night, I'm a little short of cash."

"Tell you what—level with me about who ran you off the road and why, and I'll give you a ride wherever you want to go."

"I've already leveled. I don't know the

who or the why. And what do you care, anyway?"

"Call me nosy—and law-abiding." Bart started punching numbers on his cell phone.

"Who are you calling?"

"The sheriff."

She grabbed his hand before he completed the call. "Okay, I'll tell you everything." She scanned the area. "Just not out here in the parking lot. Where's your truck?"

"A couple of rows over."

She walked with him to his vehicle, then threw herself into the passenger side and propped her duffel between them. "It's an ugly story."

"I wasn't expecting Cinderella." Though with Jaclyn, it could well be a fairy tale. "Why don't we start with your real name?"

"Jaclyn Jones." She spelled Jaclyn for him.

"I'll buy the Jaclyn part. The nurses couldn't find your driver's license last night. Where is it?"

"I left it in my other handbag."

"How convenient. What part of Louisiana are you from?"

"I'm currently living in New Orleans."

That might actually be the truth. "So what brought you to Colts Run Cross?"

"I don't see as it's any of your business, but I'm having an affair with a married man who lives in Houston. We wanted to go somewhere where we could venture out of the bedroom for a change and not risk running into anyone we knew."

"Where's the boyfriend now?"

"We got into a fight last night, and I broke it off with him. He went berserk and evidently followed me when I left the motel."

"Which motel?"

"I don't remember the name of it, just some shabby, nondescript motel. Anyway, I'm sure he's cooled down by now and is ready to beg my forgiveness."

"But not sorry enough to rent you another car or even drive you home?"

"I'm going home to my husband and putting all this behind me—at least I am if I can get there."

Bart didn't know how much, if any, of her story was true, but it would explain why she hadn't wanted to call her husband. He started the truck and backed out of the parking spot.

A few minutes later he was headed in the same direction from which he'd come, toward Jack's Bluff and the spot where she'd been run off the road last night.

"Did you talk to Hank about your friend Margo's car?" he asked.

She visibly bristled. "I don't know what you're talking about."

"The Buick was registered to a Margo Kite. I was assuming that was a friend—unless you stole the car from her."

She looked away. "Right. Margo. I'll explain everything to her when I see her again."

Her cell phone jangled. She said hello, but that was it. After that she merely listened as her muscles grew taut. Her hands were shaking by the time she broke the connection.

"Was that the boyfriend?"

"Yeah." Her shoulders slumped and she kicked off her shoes and pulled her feet onto the seat with her. "He's a jerk. So what's new?"

Neither of them spoke until he was almost to Jack's Bluff. He slowed the car as they approached the gate. The smart thing to do would be to keep driving to the bus station, but the inconsistencies were eating away at him.

The story she'd told about the lover was no more convincing than her having had amnesia. The only thing he was certain of was that someone had tried to kill her last night, and from all indications she was still afraid.

All of which was none of his business. He tried to drill that mantra into his brain but got nowhere. She was scared and distrustful but vulnerable. Dropping her off at a bus station without knowing she'd be safe seemed excessively cold and cruel for a man who stayed up all night with horses in labor and lost sleep worrying over a premature calf.

He turned left and opened the metal gate to the ranch with the remote attached to his visor.

Jaclyn snapped to attention. "Hold it right here, cowboy. I did not agree to make any unscheduled stops with you."

For a woman begging favors, she could sure climb on her high horse in a hurry. "You missed lunch at the hospital. I thought you might be hungry. And even if you're not, I am."

"Are you sure we're just stopping here for food?"

"What else would it be?"

"You're a man. I'm a woman. Surely you can figure that out."

"I wouldn't seduce you on a bet." Not exactly true, but it sounded good. The problem was he didn't know exactly what he hoped to accomplish by spending additional time with Jaclyn. He just wasn't quite ready to let it go. And he was always ready to eat.

JACLYN STARED AT THE house, which sat a few yards from where Bart had stopped the car. It was a two-story frame structure set in a clump of sycamores and oaks and a few types of trees she didn't recognize. A covered front porch ran the length of it, with a wooden swing at one end and a couple of painted rockers at the other.

There was no landscaping except the natural Texas countryside of grass, scrubby brush and a large pond a few yards behind the house, but it still looked welcoming. Maybe it was the pot of blooming begonias by the door. A fish jumped as she scanned the sun-glittered water, a streak of silver that broke the surface with a splash.

"Some bunkhouse," she said as she followed Bart to the porch.

"I like it. The menu choices will be limited, but I can rustle up a sandwich."

"A sandwich is good." She wasn't particularly hungry, but it could be a long time before she made it back to Margo's New Orleans apartment. She wouldn't be buying much in the way of food along the way. Her cash resources weren't just low, they were scratching bottom. Worse, she was no closer to the information she needed. The trip to Colts Run Cross had been a total bomb.

"The begonias are beautiful," she said as Bart opened the front door and waited for her to enter.

"Compliments of my mother. She thinks I need flowers."

"Your mom brings plants to the ranch?"

"Yeah. No reason for you not to know," Bart said. "This isn't a bunkhouse, it's my house, and Jack's Bluff Ranch belongs to my family."

"Why didn't you say that in the first place?"

"You didn't ask."

But she should have known from her first look at the tux. Apprehension swelled. The rich always stuck together. If she'd had any thought of telling Bart the truth, it was out of the question now.

"I haven't done much to the inside of the house yet," Bart said as he held the front door open for her to enter. "I mostly spend time on it in the winter when work on the ranch slows down a bit. I don't do much but sleep here in the summer. I'm usually busy until late and then grab dinner up at the big house with the rest of the family."

The big house—as if this were a cracker box. It was three times the size of her one-bedroom efficiency back in Shreveport. She looked around. The front room was empty except for a couple of recliners and a TV boxed in between bare shelves. But the windows were splendid, floor-to-ceiling and offering a pastoral vista that stretched as far as she could see.

"Nice room," she said. "I like the view."

"I don't like to feel closed in."

She followed Bart to the kitchen, keenly aware of how sexy he looked in his jeans, Western shirt and boots and how well he fit in his world. A world as different from hers as night and day.

Bart opened the door to the refrigerator while Jaclyn absorbed the ambience. She ran her hand across the top of a rectangular oak table with cuts and scratches and an abundance of character.

"My great-great-grandfather made that," Bart said. "It had been retired to a storage barn behind the original bunkhouse. I decided it needed to be rescued."

"So you don't just rescue damsels in distress?"

"I'm a softy at heart."

He looked plenty tough to her, but the idea of family belongings being passed down in any condition was a foreign concept to her. "Is the potbellied stove a family heirloom, as well?"

"It is, but notice I have an actual electric range for cooking—well, for scrambling eggs and making coffee. That's the extent of my culinary skills." Bart pulled out two packages wrapped in butcher paper. "How about a ham-and-cheese sandwich?"

"Fine. I'll be glad to help, but I need to wash up first."

"The bathroom is just down the hall, second door to your right. Excuse the unfinished walls. My sister Becky insists it should have wallpaper and keeps bringing home patterns that look like someone spilled sherbet on them."

Becky was missing the mark. Bart was clearly not a pastel kind of guy, and even unfinished, the house reeked of him. Virile. Masculine. It smelled of him, too, all outdoorsy and musky, with scents of leather and coffee thrown into the mix.

He was unlike any of the men who'd come and gone in her life, and she'd have to stay on guard every second to keep from believing he might be different enough that she could trust him. This time she couldn't screw up.

BART STARTED TO SLICE a fresh tomato but stopped to stare at the handbag Jaclyn had left on one of the kitchen chairs. The unexpected urge to snoop swelled inside him. It wasn't the kind of thing he'd normally do, but he didn't ordinarily become entangled with a woman like Jaclyn. While he was considering the action, she returned, grabbed the purse and marched back to the bathroom with it safely clutched in her hands.

He left the knife and the tomato on the table and stepped out the back door. The temperature had dropped to the low sixties, delivering the first real hint of fall. Leaves drifted to the damp earth, and a couple of crows heckled him from the branches of a hackberry tree.

He made a quick call to Langston's private number at Collingsworth Oil and was amazed when he actually got him on the first try. Langston was the mover and shaker in the family, the only one of the four brothers who'd actually taken to the business world.

"You got a minute?" he asked as soon as Langston answered.

"If it's important, I'll find one. What's up?"

"I was wondering if you'd make a call to your buddy Aidan Jefferies for me." Aidan was a homicide detective for the Houston Police Department and he and Langston had been buddies for years.

"Is there a problem at the ranch?"

"No, it's a long story, but I'm trying to run down some information on a woman who was in a wreck out this way last night. It's important and rather urgent."

"I can give you his cell phone number if you want to call him yourself."

"No, I only have a minute, but if you'd just ask him to see what he can find on a Jaclyn Jones or a Margo Kite, both of New Orleans…" He spelled Jaclyn the way she'd spelled it for him in the hospital.

"Do you have social security numbers on them?"

"No. All I can tell you is that Jaclyn is in her early twenties. And the address for Margo was…" He tried to recall the information from the registration, but all he could remember was a street name. "Margo lives on St. Anne—or at least she did at one time."

"That's not much to go on, but I'll give him a call for you."

"I'd appreciate that. Tell him he can call me back on my cell phone if he learns anything."

"You got it. I expect to hear the rest of this story when we both get a minute."

The screen door squeaked open and Jaclyn joined Bart on the back porch. "Sure thing. Right now I've gotta run." Bart broke the connection and returned the cell phone to his pocket.

"I thought you were making sandwiches," Jaclyn said, looking at him suspiciously.

"I got a call from one of my brothers."

"And I guess you had to tell him about rescuing the ditzy blonde."

"Are you ditzy?"

"Only if it suits my purpose."

She'd finally said something he believed.

"So are we going to eat or not?"

He followed her back through the screen door. In minutes they were seated at the old oak table, munching on sandwiches and chips. Bart had milk with his. Jaclyn had a diet soda. Bart tried to make conversation, but Jaclyn managed to sabotage every attempt with silent shrugs or one-word responses.

They'd finished the meal and rinsed the dishes and were walking back to the car when Aidan called back. It was quicker than Bart had anticipated.

Aidan got right to the meat of the matter. "The New Orleans PD took a missing-persons report on a Margo Kite, age twenty-three, on October seventh."

Today was October twenty-third, so they were talking just over two weeks ago. "Who filed the report?"

"A woman named Jaclyn McGregor, who claimed to be a friend. She spelled her first name the same way as your Jaclyn Jones, for what that's worth. The police took the report but virtually dismissed it, as Miss Kite had given up her apartment as of October fifteenth and told the landlady that she was leaving the area. She was reportedly unemployed."

"That's it?"

"There were two Jaclyn Joneses in New Orleans with police records—one for writing bad checks, the other for having a grand total of twenty parking tickets. One was age thirty-two, the other age forty-five."

Wrong age to be the Jaclyn staring at him now and obviously listening to his conversation. But the Jaclyn McGregor who'd filed the missing-persons report on Margo Kite had possibilities. "I appreciate the help on that."

"Want to say what this is about?"

"Not at the moment."

"Okay, then hope that helps."

"It could." He brought the call to a quick end and grabbed Jaclyn's arm so that she couldn't walk away. "That was a bit of interesting information, Jaclyn *McGregor*."

"Let go of me," she ordered, but the look on her face and the depths of her eyes told him all he needed to know.

"Why did you lie about your last name?"

"I'm a chronic fibber. I'm a procrastinator, too. And I hog the covers. Now just drop me off at the bus station and forget you ever met me. Better yet, drop me off at the highway and I'll thumb my way back to town."

"Now that's smart."

She stiffened. "What do you want from me, Bart?"

"The truth."

"So you can regale the family tonight with tales of the daring rescue of the mystery woman who'd been run off the road by a lunatic? Why don't you just go out and get a life of your own?"

"I think you're in trouble. I might be able to help."

"Well, you can't. So let it go."

"Have you found Margo Kite?"

Her eyes shadowed and she trembled. "What do you know about Margo?"

"Only that you filed a missing-persons claim. Is that why you're in Texas—to search for Margo Kite?"

Jaclyn paled. Her composure was wavering fast. "Maybe."

"There was no boyfriend last night, was there?"

She turned away.

"Tell me about your friend's disappearance, Jaclyn. I have lots of connections. I might be able to help. If not, you haven't lost anything but a few minutes of your time."

"You really don't want to get involved in this, Bart Collingsworth. You don't want to get involved with me."

He let go of her arm. "Why don't you let me be the judge of that?"

She didn't answer, but when he took her right hand in his, she let him lead her back to the porch and to the swing that creaked in the slight breeze. "Tell me one good reason I should trust you, Bart Collingsworth."

"Because from the looks of things, you don't have anyone else to go to for help. And I'm offering."

"You're making a mistake, cowboy. A monumental mistake."

Chapter Four

Jaclyn was quaking on the inside though trying desperately to keep up her facade of confidence. It was foolish to trust a man she barely knew when she'd never been able to trust anyone before, but he made a valid point, and right now it was the only one that mattered. She was desperate to find Margo, and he had the resources to help her do it.

Birds were chirping in the trees near the house, accompanied by the occasional mournful mooing of cows in the pasture beyond the pond. Jaclyn gathered her thoughts, then took a deep breath and blurted out the fact that haunted her every waking hour. "I did file a missing-persons report on my friend Margo two weeks ago. No one has seen or heard from her in over three weeks, and I know she's in some kind of trouble— or in danger."

Bart's eyes narrowed. "Has she disappeared like this before?"

"No. We kept in touch almost daily by e-mail, and she called at least once a week. And she always responded immediately if I asked her something or left a message for her to call me back."

"That seems a bit excessive for two grown women."

"This from a man whose mother brings him flowers?" The wisecrack popped out before she thought. Sarcasm was a defense mechanism she'd taken up early on and couldn't seem to break. "Look, I've had some hard times lately. Margo's the kind of friend you can count on. So when she didn't answer my SOS e-mails or phone messages to see what was up, I panicked and caught a ride to New Orleans with a coworker."

"Had she said anything to make you think she could be in trouble?"

"Just the opposite. My last e-mail message from her was on September twenty-ninth.

She wrote that things were going well and that she'd have big news for me soon."

"That's all she said."

"Yes, but I took it to mean she had a promising job offer. She hasn't worked since she was laid off from her job as a bartender at one of the restaurants in the French Quarter in August."

"Maybe she didn't get the job and hates to admit it."

"I considered that, but it's not like Margo not to stay in touch no matter what's going on. When I got to her apartment, I knew it was more. She didn't just move out. She's either on the run because she's afraid or she's been abducted or…" Or worse, but Jaclyn wasn't ready to deal with that possibility yet.

"That's a pretty extreme assumption."

"You wouldn't think that if you'd seen her apartment. It looked as if she'd stepped outside and never come back in. There was a full pot of coffee, and her computer was still on. So was the ceiling fan in her bedroom and there was a load of wet towels in the washing machine. Even her car was still there and parked in her regular parking spot."

"But no Margo?"

"Right." The fear multiplied with every word of explanation. It was just so clear that Margo had not left of her own free will.

"Did you check with the landlady or the neighbors?"

"That was the first thing I did. The landlady hadn't seen her since she gave notice on September thirtieth that she would be moving out on October fifteenth."

"You didn't mention she was moving."

"I didn't know it. I was guessing it was due to her getting the job and part of the surprise."

"What did the neighbors say?"

"There was only one. Margo lives in one of those narrow three-story buildings with apartments over a ground-level shop, so there aren't many tenants. The man who shares the third level with her told me he hadn't seen or heard her in at least two weeks. The elderly woman who has an apartment next to the landlady's on the second floor is visiting her son in San Diego and has been away since the middle of September."

"I'd have to agree with you that this

doesn't quite add up. Did you explain every-thing to the police?"

"I tried. They took the information down, but all they would focus on was that she was a legal adult who'd given notice to the manager of the apartment complex that she was moving out. They asked if there was blood in the apartment. When I said no, it seemed they lost interest."

"What about friends? A boyfriend?"

"She didn't have close girlfriends, but there is most definitely a man—a married state senator. She was convinced he was going to leave his wife and marry her."

"I take it you don't think he was."

"Do they ever?"

"I guess some must, considering the divorce rate in this country. Have you talked to the senator?"

"Of course. I got nowhere. He denied even knowing Margo. He's behind her disappear-ance—I know it. Now I just have to prove it." The fury was so strong that talking about him burned her throat.

"What's his name?" Bart asked.

"Pat Hebert."

"Patrick Lewis Hebert?"

Her nerves knotted like twisted twine at the recognition in Bart's tone. "Don't tell me he's a friend of yours."

"No, but I've met him. He and some other guys from Louisiana co-own Paradise Pastures—a small ranch about a half hour west of here—and they frequent the local bars and cafés when they're around. He seems friendly enough, especially with the women. I never got the idea that he was married."

"Not surprising since he seemed to forget that fact himself," Jaclyn said. "But if he's familiar with this area, then that proves he's the one who lured me to Colts Run Cross in the first place. He'd planned to ambush me all along."

Bart planted his feet and stopped the gentle sway of the swing. "Now we're getting somewhere. Exactly how were you lured to this area?"

"I received a phone call two days ago from someone speaking in an obviously disguised voice telling me to meet him in Cutter's Bar in Colts Run Cross last night if I wanted to find out what had happened to Margo. I showed up at the appointed time, but no one else did. I waited for two hours before I left. Apparently I was set up. He called back when I was sitting in your truck and said that if I didn't stop looking for Margo, I'd end up dead."

"You really are convinced that Hebert is behind all of this?"

"Wouldn't you be under the circumstances?"

"I'd be suspicious, but it's a big jump from suspicious to accusing a state senator of abducting a lover—or worse."

And there was no reason for him to stick his neck into that kind of noose.

"If you want out, just say so," she said, trying for flippant to cover her desperation.

"I didn't say I wanted out. I just like to have all the facts before I go accusing a politician of wrongdoing, especially of something as serious as foul play involving a mistress. Isn't it possible that they had an argument or that he broke up with her and she just took off?"

"If he had nothing to do with her disappearance, why deny they were having an affair?"

"Maybe to keep his wife from divorcing

him—or to avoid a career-ending scandal." He fingered his Stetson and tugged it a little lower on his forehead. "I'm still willing to help, but I have one condition."

She squared her shoulders. "Surprise, surprise."

"Make that two conditions. Quell the sarcasm and we do this my way, which means I call the shots."

"Why should I agree to anything?"

"Because you need my help. You were almost killed last night, and from what you've said, you haven't made much headway in finding out what's happened to your friend on your own."

"What's in this for you?"

"Did it ever occur to you that I might be doing this because it's the right thing to do?"

It had occurred to her, but she still had difficulty buying it. "So does this mean you're going to drive me back to New Orleans?" she asked.

"Are you staying in New Orleans now?"

"Yes. I talked Margo's landlady into letting me keep her apartment until the end of the month. She agreed—for a price."

Bart frowned. "And your husband went along with that?"

"He doesn't know," she said, the familiar lie surprisingly sticking in her throat. "His National Guard unit was called into action in the Middle East. He has enough to worry about without laying this on him."

"I have to take care of some things here at the ranch before I take off. The earliest I can leave is tomorrow morning. I only have one bed here at my place, but you can stay at the big house."

"With your mom?"

"And the rest of the family. There's plenty of room. And if you think you have questions about why I'm jumping into the missing-person's game, you can bet my family will have a hundred more. But don't worry—I'll give them some kind of explanation and insist they not give you the third degree."

The thought of facing the rest of the Collingsworths unsettled her to the point of nausea. She was never comfortable in family situations. They elicited too many memories, all of them bad.

"Don't worry," Bart said, no doubt reading her mind from her furrowed brow. "They'll love you."

"Sure, cowboy. About the way they'd love a copperhead curled up in the middle of their bed."

"Just don't make rattling noises," he quipped, "and they'll never know you're venomous."

BART'S PICKUP TRUCK rattled and bounced along what loosely passed for a road. Jaclyn's nerves grew more rattled with each jolt. "So exactly who will be at dinner?" she asked as the jutted roofline of what she assumed to be the big house came into view.

"Tonight it will be my mother, all three of my brothers, my two sisters, my two nephews and possibly my grandfather. He had a stroke a few months ago and he's been slow to recover. He doesn't always show up for dinner these days. And, of course, Juanita will be on the scene. She's the cook."

"Hail, hail, the gang's all here."

"Not quite. My brother Langston's wife Trish and their daughter Gina won't be there.

They live in Houston, and Gina's usually buried in homework or busy with extracurricular activities on school nights."

"How will I ever tell the players without a scorecard?"

"It'll be easy. Langston's the oldest brother, the businessman of the family. He's president of Collingsworth Oil and he'll probably come right from work, which means he'll be the only brother not wearing jeans."

"Don't tell me he drives out here from Houston every night just to eat dinner."

"No, we have some business to discuss."

Probably concerning her. This was getting worse by the second. "What about the other brothers?"

"Matt's the second oldest. If you look close, you can see a scar on the left temple where he got kicked by a bull during his brief fling in the rodeo world. He's four years older than I am."

"Which would make him?"

"Thirty-three."

"So you haven't yet reached the moldy age of thirty?"

"Not a speck of mold on my body."

She had no doubt that was true, though she had no plans to inspect for proof. Physical intimacy with a man like Bart would be a shortcut to heartbreak. She'd run the risk of falling hard, and once he found out the truth about her past, he'd dump her as if she were a mad cow carrier.

"That leaves one more brother," she said.

"Zach, the baby of the family along with my sister Jaime. They're twins. Zach is a ladies' man and a practical joker. Jaime's the free spirit—Mother's polite way of saying she's never met a rule she couldn't break."

"I already like her best."

"Somehow I knew you would. My sister Becky is separated from her husband Nick, a pro football player who everyone gets along with except Becky. She says they have issues. I think that means Nick prefers taking orders from his coach instead of from Becky, but I try not to get involved."

"Good idea. Are Becky and Nick the parents of your two nephews?"

"Right. David and Derrick are twins, seven years old, mischievous and have boundless energy. Watch out for toads in your bed."

"Thanks for the warning. And your mom?"

"Lenora Collingsworth. She's fifty-six and runs circles around all of us. When Jeremiah had his stroke, he shocked us all by having papers drawn up that turned the position of CEO of Collingsworth Enterprises over to her at any point he couldn't fulfill the required duties.

"The only paying job she'd ever had before was as a waitress before she got married. But she's amazed us all with her tenacity and ability, though she drives Langston a little nuts with her reforms for the oil company. Collingsworth Enterprises includes ranch operations, but she hasn't gotten to telling us how to run Jack's Bluff yet."

"Collingsworth Oil, Collingsworth Enterprises, Jack's Bluff Ranch. You sound like the Ewings of Southfork."

"More scruples and a lot fewer sexual escapades."

And in spite of the wealth, Bart still appeared to be just an easygoing cowboy with no hidden agenda. But that didn't mean the same would be true of the rest of his family. Lenora especially worried her. A woman astute enough to step into the role of CEO without prior executive experience would surely see through Jaclyn. She'd know instinctively that Jaclyn was bad news for her son. She'd be right.

Bart pulled into the drive behind a row of pickups, a Porsche, a BMW, a silver Mercedes and a Harley. But it was the sprawling house, not the impressive vehicles, that claimed her attention. It wasn't elaborate. There were no ostentatious columns or intricate masonry. There were only gables and porches and huge oak trees embracing the structure. It was homey and welcoming—at least that was the illusion it created.

She was hit with a paralyzing attack of nerves. "I can't do this, Bart."

"Can't do what?"

"Intrude on your family."

"You're not intruding, you're an invited guest."

"But they don't know me. For that matter, neither do you."

"We're feeding you, not adopting you. Just relax."

One of his brothers walked out the back

door and waved. Bart waved back. She gritted her teeth, climbed reluctantly from the car and followed Bart to the house.

"SHE'S WOW MATERIAL," Zach said. "Not sure you can handle a sweet, young hottie like that, big brother, even if she is the size of a good bottle of tequila."

Bart poured himself a mug of coffee and leaned against the kitchen counter. "I told you—she's married to a serviceman. I have no plans to 'handle' her. I'm just going to drive her back to New Orleans and see if her friend's disappearance checks out to be as suspicious as she fears."

"And if it is?" Matt asked.

"Then I'll see what I can do to help her find out what happened to the missing woman."

Zach opened the refrigerator and pulled out a half-gallon container of milk. "Politicians being what they are today, it wouldn't surprise me a bit if Hebert is involved in her disappearance."

"Whether he is or not, I suspect he's anxious to keep his affair away from public scrutiny," Langston said. "But he's going pretty far if he's the one guilty of running— or having Jaclyn run—off the road last night."

"Desperate situations call for desperate measures," Bart countered. "And if he's guilty of foul play, the guy is not only desperate and immoral but also depraved."

"Which would put Jaclyn in serious danger," Langston admitted.

Bart had especially requested Langston's presence at the informal after-dinner confab. Langston wasn't as negative as Matt or as impulsive as Zach and he was used to dealing with difficult situations and political confrontations in the business world.

"So what do you suggest, Langston?"

"I'd say the first step is to hire a good private investigator. I put Clay Markham on retainer for Collingsworth Oil a couple of months ago, so you're welcome to use him. He's as good as they come. I'd suggest having a background check done on Jaclyn, as well. She seems nice, but appearances can be deceiving. And then I'd make a personal visit to the Louisiana senator who's suspected of foul play."

Zach cut himself a slice of chocolate cake to go with his milk, scattering crumbs as he took it from the cake plate to a napkin. "Foul play? You sound like a politician yourself. Just say it like it is. There's a good chance Margo was murdered. Then you can get down to the nitty-gritty of finding out who, why and where."

Bart shook his head. "Don't let Jaclyn hear you say that. She's still hoping for the best."

Matt rocked back on the heels of his boots, his face grim. "Did it ever occur to you that this Margo woman could have blackmailed the senator, then taken off with the money? The way I see it, that's the most likely scenario. If it were me, I'd buy Jaclyn a plane ticket home, maybe even offer to pay for a private detective for her since you said her husband's off fighting for our country. Then I'd ride off into the sunset like a smart cowboy."

"I'll drive her home," Bart said. "After that, I may follow your advice." But he doubted it. There was something about Jaclyn and the situation that had hold of him, and he just couldn't see himself letting go of it until he had more facts.

He'd have to be careful around Jaclyn for the reason Zach had said. She was wow material. And she was married. But she was also spunky and possibly in real danger. He couldn't just turn his back on her.

"Keep us posted," Langston said. "And don't take any unnecessary risks."

"Don't worry. The image of dead hero has no appeal for me."

"And keep your pants zipped and your heart in tow," Zach cautioned. "Jaclyn's the kind of woman who could burrow under a man's skin without even trying."

"I have the skin of an armadillo," Bart said, though he wasn't sure even that was tough enough to avoid letting Jaclyn get to him. Still, he'd never messed with another man's wife before—and he damn sure wouldn't start with the wife of a serviceman on active duty.

Bart and his brothers joined their mother and their sister Becky on the screened back porch for Langston to say his goodbyes.

"Where are Jaime and Jaclyn?" Bart

asked, alarmed that Jaime might be somewhere bombarding her with questions.

"Jaime went into town with a couple of her
girlfriends," Lenora said. "Jaclyn seemed
tired, so I suggested she go upstairs and get
some rest. She seemed grateful for the offer."

"That's probably a good idea," Bart
agreed, hating the disappointment that he
hadn't gotten to tell her good-night.

"She's really worried about her friend,"
Becky said. "She didn't say much, but I
could hear it in her voice when she talked
about the police blowing off her concerns."

Lenora stood and walked over to where
Bart was standing. "I don't know how the
police can do that. I know the area's had a hard
time coming back after Katrina and that the
police have their hands full with the upswing
in crime, but surely they could have at least
questioned people about her disappearance."

"It's hard to say what they were thinking
or what they've actually done," Bart said,
"but I think the situation deserves better than
it's getting."

"I'm not sure you're getting involved in
this is a good idea, Bart."

He dropped an arm around his mother's shoulders. "Aren't you the one who always says that the Lord expects us to reach out to those in need?"

"Don't twist my words around, Bart. Jaclyn needs police assistance, and you're not in law enforcement."

"I've seen all the episodes of *Law & Order.*"

"This isn't a joking matter."

He knew that all too well. "I don't plan on doing anything stupid or reckless. I'll be fine, Mom. Now tell me about your day," he said, eager to change the subject. "Langston says you're researching the possibility of child care for the employees of Collingsworth Oil who have young children."

She clearly wasn't convinced his going to New Orleans with Jaclyn was a good idea, but she was eager to talk about her plans. He listened a good fifteen minutes, then excused himself to go back to his place and get some sleep.

He was walking through his front door when he got a call from Aidan Jefferies.

"I hate to call you this late, but I've been

out at the crime scene of an armed robbery at a convenience store in southeast Houston. The clerk was shot twice in the head, but we've got a good lead on the perp. Anyway, I'd asked one of the young recruits to see what he could find on Jaclyn McGregor, since that was the name given by the woman who reported Margo Kite's disappearance."

"What did he find?"

"A good reason for you to say *adios.*"

Bart's blood boiled as he listened to the details of Jaclyn's recent past. He swallowed the curses that flew to mind as he thanked Aidan and headed back to his car. He had a few words for Jaclyn, and they wouldn't wait until morning.

Chapter Five

Jaclyn had retired to her room at the Collingsworths' early, but not because she was exhausted, as she'd claimed. The family camaraderie and familiarity had made her increasingly uneasy. They had tried to make her feel welcome, but that was only because they didn't know the real Jaclyn McGregor.

So she'd escaped to the guest room and sat here alone. Voices had drifted from downstairs for a while, but it was quiet now, and when she'd heard a truck leaving earlier, she'd looked out the window and seen that it was Bart.

He'd be back at his house by the pond by now, probably with his window open so that the drone of the crickets and the rustle of leaves dancing in the breeze lulled him into a sound sleep. All was well at Jack's Bluff.

But all was not well with Margo. Jaclyn usually managed to hold on to her optimism during the day. But when night came, there was no holding back the nightmarish possibilities that crept into her mind. No one understood her certainty that Margo was in trouble, but she knew it as surely as she knew that day would follow night—or that Bart would soon find out about her past and drop her, possibly even en route back to New Orleans.

Jaclyn slipped her shirt over her head and dropped it to the bed, then reached behind her to unsnap her bra. She may as well grab a shower and try to get some sleep. She hadn't brought pajamas with her, but there were white chenille guest robes in the closet, so she'd slip on one of them to traipse to the bathroom just down the hall.

She'd just unsnapped her jeans when a loud and very persistent knock sounded at the door. She rushed to the closet, slipped into the robe and opened the door just wide enough to peek out. Bart glared back at her, then pushed his way into the room without waiting for an invitation.

"We need to talk."

His tone told her everything. He knew who and what she was.

He stepped in front of her, crowding her space. "I don't like being played the fool, Jaclyn."

"You have a short memory, Bart. You're the one who insisted I come home with you."

"Why didn't you tell me you had a criminal record?"

She stood her ground in spite of her sinking spirit. "I did my time. I'm just a citizen now, same as you."

She ducked under his arm and walked to the bed, wrapping both hands around the bedpost. She tried to keep up her tough exterior, but her facade was crumbling fast. "What exactly did you hear?"

"That you did two years in a women's prison in Louisiana for theft and that you were only released a little over a month ago."

"So there you have the lurid details of my life." Two years in prison that had seemed a lifetime. Two years of humiliation and fear that she'd cross the wrong inmate and end up being brutalized as the day's entertainment.

"I'm an ex-con, so you can kick me out anytime it suits you. Or do you shoot criminals around here?"

"Did you steal the money from your boss?"

"A jury said that I did."

"Drop the sarcasm, Jaclyn."

"Why? Because you're a Collingsworth? Because you're some holier-than-thou Good Samaritan?" Pain shot up her arms, and when she looked down she saw that her knuckles had whitened at the death grip she held on the bedpost. She took a deep breath and tried to rein in her emotions. "What does it matter what I say now, Bart? You're not going to believe me."

His muscles were bunched and taut, and she could see the flex of his biceps beneath his shirtsleeves. He didn't meet her gaze, and she looked away as the hurt ground inside her. She should have known he was no different from everyone else.

"Drive me to the highway, Bart. I'll thumb a ride into town."

He didn't respond, and she started stuffing the few items she'd unpacked back into her duffel. She yanked the zipper to close it, then swallowed a curse when the metal teeth caught on a swatch of bunched fabric. She bit her bottom lip, determined to hold back the tears as frustration pushed her past the point of stability.

"Let me help you with you that."

"No." The refusal flew from her lips. "I don't need your help. I don't need anyone's help."

Before she could back away, Bart pulled her into his arms, and the ridiculous tears pushed from her eyes. After all she'd been through over the past years, why did she have to fall apart now? "I don't need your pity, Bart. Just take me to the highway, and I'll be out of your life for good."

He lifted her chin so that she had to meet his gaze. "We'll decide that later. Right now I just need to get some things straight."

Her body steadied, but the trembling merely moved deeper inside her, rolling in her stomach and rattling her nerves. "I'm an ex-con, Bart. Nothing I say will change that. So if you're looking for a sweet, innocent damsel to rescue, you'll have to keep looking."

"I was never looking to begin with."

BART HAD NEVER EVEN considered dumping Jaclyn on the highway, but he had been fuming when he'd hung up the phone with Aidan. Now he was floundering, still angry but also drawn to Jaclyn in a way that made no sense. He knew she'd lied to him over and over again, yet in spite of everything, he found himself aching to comfort her.

Jaclyn pulled away from him and took a seat on the edge of the mattress. Her shoulders were squared, her back straight, the kind of spunk she'd have needed to endure two years in a state pen. But the rest of her showed nothing but vulnerability.

"Is what you told me about Margo's disappearance actually the truth?" he asked, knowing he had to get at least that much clear in his mind.

"Yes. I would never lie about that. And I don't expect you to believe me, but I didn't steal the money from my boss, either. I was set up by his son who managed the restaurant for him."

"Why?"

"He wanted sexual favors from me. I refused and he became furious. I expected to be fired. Instead he stole cash from the restaurant safe on a night when the two of us worked the late shift and were in charge of locking up."

"There must have been more evidence than just the fact that you had opportunity."

"Oh, there was plenty of evidence. A bank deposit bag full of money taken from the safe was found in my car."

"Did your employer's son have a key to your car?"

"Apparently—but I didn't give it to him. I suspect he took mine from my handbag while I was working and had a duplicate made."

"How much money are we talking about?"

"Just under ten thousand dollars."

"And all of it was recovered?"

"No, only three thousand was in the bank deposit bag when the police searched my car at Ellis Gravier's suggestion. They found it stashed beneath the backseat. That was three days after the money went missing."

"I take it Ellis Gravier was the son in question."

"Right. His father offered to drop the

charges if I repaid everything, but there was no way I could get my hands on that kind of money. I had an academic scholarship to the university, but it only paid for tuition. The rest of my living expenses had to come out of my salary from the restaurant and my school loans and grants. I had no savings and no collateral for a loan."

"Where was your husband while this was going on?"

"He…he wasn't around."

"And you had no family who could help you out?"

"No, nor did I have money to hire the caliber of attorney the Graviers produced."

Bart didn't doubt that part of her story. The rich did have an advantage in the court system. And he could definitely imagine the boss's son craving sexual favors from Jaclyn.

Bart pictured Jaclyn behind bars, sharing living space with the worst of humanity, enduring who knew what. His blood ran cold at the thought.

"Don't worry, Bart. I don't expect you to honor your offer of help now. We have so little in common we may as well be from different planets."

He dropped to the bed beside her. "Looks like the planets have collided now, so we may as well make the most of it."

She raked her hair back from her face and tucked the feathered locks behind her ears before she turned to face him. "Does that mean that you still want to help with my search for Margo?"

The answer was complicated, but that was about the size of it. Only it wasn't so much that he *wanted* to help her but that he felt *compelled* to help her—and had since he'd first pulled her from the wrecked car.

Still, the nagging doubts ground in his stomach, and he didn't want to promise more than he could deliver. "I'll drive you to New Orleans and do what I can."

"Are you sure?" Her voice was tentative.

"Yeah, Jaclyn. I'm sure." He hoped he sounded more positive than he felt. "Now you need to get some sleep. I do, too. In fact, I'll just crash in the guest room down the hall and wake you for an early start."

He walked to the door.

"Wait, Bart."

He turned and looked back at her. She twisted her wedding band, then pulled it off and dropped it to the bed beside her. "While I'm leveling with you, I may as well go all the way. I'm not married. I've never been married."

"Then why the ring?"

"Sometimes it keeps guys like Ellis Gravier from hitting on me. Sometimes not."

"So there's no husband fighting for the country?"

"No."

"Why are you telling me this now?"

"You'd find out sooner or later. You're obviously having me investigated. I'm merely trying to avoid having you fly off the handle again."

He nodded and swallowed hard. Believing she was married had been an asset, kind of like an insurance policy to make certain he didn't let himself get too emotionally involved with her. Now he'd lost that protection and he knew he'd have to keep up his guard every second to keep the unwanted attraction for her under control.

"I just told you so you have things

straight," she said. "I don't expect it to change anything between us."

"Right." It didn't change a thing. He tried to convince himself he'd made the right decision to go with Jaclyn to New Orleans as he walked down the hall and collapsed onto the bed. He was dead tired, but he was fairly certain that sleep would be a long time in coming. Still, he was better off staying here so that he'd hear if Jaclyn decided to go on another car-theft escapade during the night and drive back to New Orleans on her own.

As it turned out, he was still awake when the grandfather clock in the downstairs hallway struck two.

BART HAD PUSHED THE speed limit making the drive from Jack's Bluff to New Orleans, so it took only minutes over six hours including stops for a fast-food breakfast, diet sodas and refueling. For at least a half hour of the trip Jaclyn had been on the phone with Clay Markham, giving the private investigator a complete rundown on Margo Kite.

Conversation between Bart and Jaclyn had been minimal and strained, except when the talk had centered on Margo. And the more they talked about Margo's disappearance, the less convinced Bart was that she'd actually met with foul play.

She might have been the one friend to stand by Jaclyn during her incarceration, but she sounded downright flaky to Bart. She was a knockout in the looks department—at least she was in the snapshot Jaclyn carried of her. But from what Jaclyn had told Clay Markham, it sounded as though Margo changed jobs, boyfriends, apartments, cities and hair color almost as frequently as normal people changed their bedsheets.

Yet Jaclyn was convinced Margo hadn't just tired of Senator Hebert and New Orleans and moved on to the next adventure. And the one thing Bart couldn't explain away was that someone had deliberately run Jaclyn off the road the other night after luring her to Colts Run Cross to talk about Margo.

The fact that it had happened practically in his backyard rankled him all the more. If Pat Hebert was involved in this, Bart would make certain the senator would be sorry he hadn't kept his dirty work at home. There were enough yellow-belly snakes in Texas without taking in exports from Louisiana.

Bart took the exit to the Vieux Carré. "You'll have to give me directions from here."

"Turn right at the intersection. Then make the first right you come to after that."

Bart hadn't been to New Orleans since he'd made the trip with a bunch of his buddies for Mardi Gras his senior year in college. He hadn't seen much that trip except Bourbon Street and the bevy of young women revealing their breasts for strings of cheap plastic beads. He and his friends had drunk way too much, and the two-day hangover he'd returned to the University of Texas with was about all he remembered of the trip.

It was a lot calmer today. There were a few tourists on the streets with their cameras slung over their necks and to-go cups of booze in hand. But for the most part the people walking along the narrow sidewalks looked to be businessmen who'd left their offices along Poydras Street to get some exercise during the noon hour or grab a bite to eat. He lowered the window to absorb the sounds and smells of the city.

He stopped at a traffic light. A homeless woman pushed a mangled grocery cart probably holding her worldly belongings across the street in front of him. The sound of a calliope from one of the paddle wheelers on the nearby Mississippi River serenaded them, along with the trumpet solo of a street musician.

"I thought the city might have changed more after Katrina," he said. "It still seems much the same."

"The French Quarter wasn't flooded," Jaclyn said. "The areas that were have been slow to recover. Two blocks down and take a left."

"We seem to be going in circles."

"We are, in a way. All the Vieux Carré streets are one-way, so there's seldom a direct route to anywhere."

The area changed from the tawdry line of souvenir and T-shirt shops to a neighborhood of crowded buildings strung with ornate balconies dripping with bougainvillea and greenery. An open doorway between two buildings offered a glimpse of a fountain in a half-hidden courtyard. The smell of shrimp from a corner café where diners were eating alfresco produced a hunger pang or two.

"The apartment is in the next block," Jaclyn said.

"Where do you park around here?" Bart asked after a quick scan didn't reveal a single open spot along the curb.

"Anyplace you can find a spot. There's a big lot down by the French Market, and most of the hotels have parking spots you can rent, but I usually just circle until I find a free space."

"I thought you said Margo had a designated parking spot."

"Margo did. She lost it when she didn't pay the bill on the first of the month. The only reason the car hadn't been towed before I arrived on the seventh was the ten-day grace period."

"I'm not crazy about leaving my truck on the street." But he would for now, he decided as he spotted a place in front of him. He backed into the spot. It was a tight fit, and with visions of new dents to his truck playing in his head, he decided he'd make better parking arrangements after this.

Bart grabbed Jaclyn's small duffel and his larger one out of the truck and followed her the half block to an iron door that opened to a steep and dimly lit staircase. She fit her key into the lock, and the door squeaked open.

"The apartment's on the third floor," Jaclyn said. "It's a steep climb. Would you like me to take my duffel?"

"No, just call for a paramedic if I pass out from lack of oxygen. Can't see how anyone lives cooped up like this."

"This isn't that bad. It's just that you're used to having acres and acres to yourself."

"As it should be."

The steps were only wide enough to take single file, which left Bart with the view of Jaclyn's noteworthy backside to focus on as he made the climb. A new wave of awareness and a twinge of arousal set in immediately.

He'd fought the feelings all morning, but it had been impossible to sit next to her in the truck for hours and not be affected by the sight, the smell and the raw sensuality that radiated from her like smoke from a smoldering campfire.

Her clothes weren't the kind you'd typically classify as unduly seductive, though the jeans did hug her bottom nicely. The blue cotton sweater she wore was neither low-cut nor too tight but merely draped her breasts so that every time he'd glanced her way all morning he'd been aware of the perky nipples beneath the fabric.

But it was the intriguing overall effect of her that really got to him. Short blond hair that fell in disheveled layers about her face, and eyes that turned from blue to gray—smoky beneath her long, lush lashes. The full, pouty lips with their soft, glistening shine that fairly screamed to be kissed didn't help either.

The twinge of arousal upgraded to a painful throb. He'd deal with it, even if it meant taking a dozen cold showers a day. Finding out she was single might have removed her from the forbidden list, but a woman like Jaclyn could make a man's libido check in and leave his brains behind. Bart didn't need that.

"What do you plan to do first?" Jaclyn

asked as they rounded the second landing and started toward the third.

"Lunch sounds good."

"Don't you cowboys think about anything but food?"

"I'm pretty much addicted to three meals a day—and used to a more satisfying breakfast than an overcooked sausage patty sandwiched between layers of doughy biscuit."

"There's no food to speak of at Margo's and no Jaunita to do the cooking."

"But there's at least one restaurant a block in the French Quarter. A bowl of seafood gumbo or crawfish étouffée could make me *temporarily* forget Juanita."

"Then I think you should eat fast and that we make a call on Senator Hebert as soon as you finish. I got nowhere with him, but he'll be a lot less likely to blow off someone with clout."

Bart wasn't at all sure he had any clout with a Louisiana senator, but it sounded good. Voices drifted down from the third floor. At least two men, maybe more, and the sound of something scraping against wood.

"Someone's in Margo's apartment," Jaclyn announced.

He'd have expected the alarm in her voice to be accompanied by at least a small measure of caution, but Jaclyn went flying up the remaining steps, not even breathing heavily from the climb.

He took off after her. One look at the two burly men staring them in the face and he figured the gumbo would have to wait.

Chapter Six

Jaclyn stormed into the room and jumped up to perch on top of the unpainted dresser the two beefy, tattooed men were carrying toward the front door. The man on the right dropped his end with such force she bounced and slid into him. The sweat and grime beaded around his neck sent her scrambling to put some distance between them.

"What do you think you're doing?" she demanded from her position a couple of feet away.

"What does it look like?" the other man said, his muscles barely flexed though he was still holding up his end of the dresser.

"Where is the rest of the furniture that was in this apartment?"

"We already carried it over to Goodwill—

same place this is going as soon as we get it on the truck."

"Then you can just go get every piece and bring it back."

"Sorry, lady, but you're not the one who writes my check. I take orders from the boss man, and he said move everything that isn't nailed down."

"Your boss has made a big mistake."

"Is this your apartment?"

"No, but..." She hesitated, knowing she had no actual authority but not ready to admit it. "I'm living here now."

He finally eased his end of the dresser back to the floor, but he was scowling as if he'd like to chew her up and spit her out.

Jaclyn scanned the room again. All Margo owned were a few pieces of worn furniture that looked as if they had been purchased at one of the secondhand stores down on Magazine Street. Now half of that was missing, including the sofa and a bookshelf.

She walked to the bedroom door and peered inside. It was totally empty. This was absurd. She'd paid the landlady to the end of the month. The woman had no right to give Margo's furniture away.

"Who instructed you to return the furniture?" Bart asked.

One of the movers reached into his pocket, took out a sheet of yellow paper and handed it to Bart, a cooperative move he hadn't extended to Jaclyn. "This is all my boss gave me. Says to move the furniture out of the house and deliver it to Goodwill Industries. Someone had already talked to them, and they were expecting it."

"How did you get in here?" Jaclyn demanded.

"Lady downstairs gave us the key. Mrs. Elway. Said she's the landlady. She knew we were coming, too, so if you got a problem, why don't you take it up with her."

"Believe me, I will."

Bart handed her the sheet of paper the mover had come up with. "You might want to take a look at this."

Her gaze fastened on the name of the hiring individual. Margo Kite. Her insides churned. There had to be some kind of mistake. If Margo were in a position to make decisions about furniture, she'd have answered Jaclyn's e-mails or returned her phone calls.

She tossed the paper to the top of the dresser. "I'm going downstairs to talk to Mrs. Elway. Don't so much as touch anything in this room until I get back."

"Then make it snappy, lady. We got a pool table to move over on the West Bank after we finish here, and the boss don't like paying overtime."

Jaclyn raced down the staircase, aware that Bart was right behind her and probably thinking she'd gone mad. But a name on a piece of paper didn't change things.

Senator Hebert was behind this. He'd gotten rid of Margo and now he planned to get rid of her furniture. He wanted no evidence left that she hadn't just moved on. But Margo wasn't disposable, like a toy that he'd played with and grown tired of. No—like a mistress who could cause complications for him.

Fury and fear collided in her mind and had her so shaky she could barely breathe as she hammered her fist on Mrs. Elway's door. The door opened a crack, but the safety latch remained fastened.

Mrs. Elway peered at her over the rims of her narrow reading glasses. "Oh, it's you, Jaclyn. I'm glad you're back, dear. I finally heard from Margo. You can stop worrying about her."

Jaclyn's pulse raced. "You talked to Margo?"

"Well, not directly." She detached the safety latch and opened the door a bit wider. "She called when I was out for my walk this morning, but she left a message on the answering machine."

"What did she say?"

"She didn't think her furniture was worth moving out of state, so she'd hired some local movers to clear out the apartment. They came about an hour ago."

"But I'm staying in the apartment."

"I know. I would have called, but I couldn't find your cell phone number." Mrs. Elway's gaze went to Bart, and she smiled appreciatively and patted her short mat of frizzy brown hair. "I don't think we've met."

"I'm Bart Collingsworth," he said, introducing himself. He extended his hand, and Mrs. Elway wrapped both of hers around his much larger one.

"And I'm Janice Elway. Are you a friend of Margo's, as well?"

"Not exactly, ma'am, but I know how worried Jaclyn's been about not being able to reach her. Would it be too much trouble for us to listen to the message?"

"Of course not. Come on in," she said, moving back for them to enter. "The machine's in the bedroom."

Jaclyn followed behind the two of them, amazed at how Bart's good looks and cowboy manners had Janice Elway smiling and holding in her stomach.

Jaclyn barely noticed the surroundings as they made their way through the living room and down a narrow hallway to what must be Mrs. Elway's bedroom. She wanted desperately to believe that the message was actually from Margo and that it would alleviate her fears, but the dread was swelling inside her, almost like a premonition that she wouldn't like what she'd hear.

The bedroom, like the rest of the house,

suited Mrs. Elway. It was a kind of aging Southern classic with a hint of last century's romanticism. The bed was cast iron, the headboard filigreed, the covering a quilt in an heirloom pattern that Jaclyn had seen before in catalogs. Vases of faded silk flowers graced the dresser, and the top of the bureau was lined with figurines whose glossy painted faces were filtered through a layer of dust.

Mrs. Elway went right to the telephone. "The connection wasn't great, but I didn't have any difficulty making out the message." She pushed a button, then stood back and waited. The playback hissed and crackled like a lightning storm before a soft female voice started talking.

"This is Margo Kite, Mrs. Elway. Sorry I didn't get a chance to say goodbye, but I've decided not to waste the money needed to move my old furniture and belongings out of state. I've called a local moving company who'll clear out the apartment for me. I didn't feel right leaving that for you." The connection crackled again, and the last few words became lost in the sputter.

Jaclyn swallowed hard as the premonition turned to a hard, black certainty. "That wasn't Margo."

"It must have been, dear. The reception was bad, but I heard her name distinctly. And the movers are here, just like she said."

"It was her name," Jaclyn agreed. "It was not her voice."

Bart snaked an arm around Jaclyn's shoulder. "Could you play it again?" he asked.

"There's no reason to play it again," Jaclyn insisted, hating that the trembling inside her had sneaked into her voice. "I know that wasn't her."

Mrs. Elway looked from Jaclyn to Bart, then restarted the recording. Someone had gone to great trouble to get Margo's slight drawl right. They'd even pronounced *fun-chur* the same way Margo did. But the intonation and cadence were wrong. Jaclyn had heard Margo's phone voice far too often not to recognize it.

"Regardless of what the caller said, that wasn't Margo."

Mrs. Elway turned off the machine and stood back, but the smile had disappeared from her thin lips. "It sounds like her to me, and the furniture has been moved out. I'm sorry, Jaclyn, but if you remain in New Orleans, you'll have to find another place to stay."

"I've already paid you through the end of the month."

"I know, but it wasn't like we had a formal lease, and I didn't think you'd want to stay with not even a bed to sleep on. Besides, one of my son's friends just called. He's separating from his wife and he needs a place he can move into this weekend. I told him he could have the apartment." She went to the bureau and opened the top drawer. "I have your refund for the remainder of the month right here."

"Do you have caller ID?" Bart asked.

"I do," Mrs. Elway said as she handed the check to Jaclyn, "but I wasn't here to see the number when it displayed."

"It should be on the call log. Do you mind if I take a look?"

"Go ahead," she said, "but the apartment is still rented."

Bart went to the on-screen menu and then to the call log. Jaclyn leaned over for a better look. Margo's number did not come up.

"Can you identify the callers?" Bart asked, moving back so that Mrs. Elway could get a better look as he scrolled down the most recent entries.

"Sure. That's Blake Melancon. He's the new tenant."

He scrolled to the next name.

"Sam Elway is my son and...Dorothy Slagen is my sister." Mrs. Elway leaned closer and squinted at the next number. "'Unavailable.' Hmm. I guess that one was the call from Margo. It must say unavailable because she's calling from out of state or because it's a new listing."

Or it was from someone who knew how to hide the number. It all added up. This was some diabolical scheme to make it look as if Jaclyn's claim that Margo had simply disappeared was ludicrous.

"Margo didn't make that call," Jaclyn insisted.

"But we thank you anyway," Bart said, shooting Jaclyn a look that warned she'd said enough. He extended a hand to Mrs. Elway. "It was a real pleasure to meet you."

"I wish I'd been here to talk to Margo," she

said. "That would have cleared all this up. She was a nice tenant, but her move didn't surprise me a'tal'."

"Really?" Bart questioned. "Why is that?"

"She didn't seem the type to stay in one place too long. Not much in the way of references, and she didn't have anything but a bed when she moved in here. I think someone gave her the rest of her furniture. I told the police that when they asked me about her."

That got Jaclyn's attention. "When were the police here?"

"Right after you showed up and started asking questions," she said as if Jaclyn should have known that. "Didn't I tell you? They said you'd been to see them."

"No, you never mentioned it."

Mrs. Elway shrugged and clasped her hands in front of her. "Guess I had one of those senior moments. They come all too frequently these days."

The thought that the police had followed up on Margo's disappearance should make Jaclyn feel better, but it didn't, not when they hadn't even bothered to get back to her. Even if they'd made some kind of perfunctory check, they'd probably given up by now, especially after talking to Mrs. Elway.

"Thanks again for letting us hear the message," Bart said, heading toward the door. "And you have a lovely home."

Mrs. Elway beamed at the compliment. Jaclyn managed to mutter a feeble attempt at appreciation, but she was dealing with a sinking sensation and the feeling that Margo was slipping away into nothingness.

Margo had been cheated out of a family, grown up without having anyone who really cared about her. Jaclyn knew the pain and emptiness of that all too well. But she would not stand by and let Margo just be erased from life. She couldn't—no matter the risks.

IT WAS AN HOUR LATER when Bart and Jaclyn finally ducked into a corner café, where the pungent odors of spices and garlic clogged the air and started an anticipatory rumble in Bart's stomach. The search for Margo had made an unexpected turn, and he had to do some regrouping in his mind to decide where to go from here.

Jaclyn was clearly convinced that hadn't been Margo's voice on the telephone, and he had no reason to doubt her instincts. She and Margo seemed as close as sisters, and he figured he'd be able to discriminate his siblings' voices from that of an impostor.

A waitress sashayed by them carrying heaping platters of fried seafood. The odors alone were enough to make his mouth water.

"Sit anywhere you can find a spot," the waitress said.

That turned out to be a small table by the back wall. The only alternative was an even smaller table directly in the path of the kitchen door. Bart pulled out a chair for Jaclyn, then took the one to her left. It at least offered a view of the front door and made him feel not quite as closed in. Somehow the whole French Quarter seemed like a big box to him, with too many walls, no hint of a breeze and not enough sunshine. To say he missed Jack's Bluff would be the understatement of the century.

If the lack of open space bothered anyone else, they were hiding it well. The laughter and loud talking indicated this was party time. The spirit of New Orleans, he guessed. The spirit did not extend to their table. Jaclyn's mood had grown continuously darker since they'd arrived in the city.

The waitress stopped by and handed them a couple of grease-stained menus. Jaclyn didn't even glance at hers before laying it aside.

"You have to eat," he said.

"I'll get a salad and some water."

"I'm paying."

"You don't have to."

"Sure I do. I'm a Texan. We have this pride thing. Goes back to the Alamo, I think."

"In that case…" She picked up her menu.

His cell phone rang. It was Langston, which likely meant he'd talked to his good buddy Aidan Jefferies and had heard about Jaclyn's past. Still, Bart was eager to talk to him. His brother had good instincts, and right now Bart could use all the savvy input he could get.

He took the call. "Hold on a sec." He turned to Jaclyn. "Excuse me," he said. "I need to take this outside, where I can hear. Order me one of those platters of seafood like the waitress was toting when we came in. And a big glass of iced tea."

She nodded, and he made his way through the maze of tables and back onto the street. "We'd just stopped for lunch," he said by way of explanation, "and I didn't want to have this conversation in front of Jaclyn."

"Good thinking. I just got off the phone with Aidan."

"I guess he told you about Jaclyn's past problems with the law."

"He said she's done time for theft."

"Yeah. She claims she didn't do the deed."

"And you believe her?"

"I don't know. Yeah, I guess I do, but to tell you the truth, her past really isn't the issue here. It's her friend's disappearance, and I'm getting really bad feelings about that."

"Have you talked to Pat Hebert?"

"Not yet." Bart filled Langston in on the movers and the mystery phone call. "Someone's trying too hard to make this look like Margo chose to drop out of sight. Pair that with Jaclyn's being run off the road and what do you get?"

"I'd say an issue that you need to drop at the well-trodden feet of the NOPD."

"I'm starting to lean in that direction

myself, but I want to talk to the senator in person first."

"Tread lightly."

"I'm not afraid of him."

"Hell, no. But you don't want to come on too strong at first. Let him think he's the smart one. That false sense of superiority is what leads the opponent to make mistakes."

"Is that from the Collingsworth Oil Executive Guidebook?"

"Either that, a Spider-Man movie or an old *Star Trek* episode. I can never remember which. But seriously, bro, watch your back. And use your resources. Backup and bodyguard services, if you need them. And most definitely use Clay Markham. He's one of the best private detectives in the business. He can dig up things about Hebert even his shadow doesn't know. And he can get the full scoop on Margo and Jaclyn."

"He's already on the job."

They finished the conversation and Bart thought he would check in with Clay Markham while he was at it. He decided to try his office first, and luckily, connected.

"I was about to call you," Clay said. "I've

been gathering info on your boy Hebert. I love investigating politicians. They are such fascinatingly decadent subjects."

"What did you find out?"

"For starters, he has taken women other than his wife to the Paradise Pastures Ranch on several occasions. That's all I can get on that so far, but I'm working on a source up there who's still a bit leery of talking to me."

"Then we know Pat Hebert strays."

"There's more. I found out that both Margo Kite and Senator Hebert were on the same flight to Puerto Vallarta, Mexico, the first week in September, though they were not listed as traveling together, nor did they sit together. He went first-class. She went coach."

"Knows how to keep 'em in their place. No wonder Margo loved him."

"Yeah. You got a pen on you?"

"I do. Hold on a minute." Bart pulled a pen from his shirt pocket and a business card from his wallet. He listened and scribbled down the information Clay gave him, including the personal data of Hebert's age, address, phone number, etc., right down to the color, make and license plate number of his car.

"Thanks for the fast work."

"I'm flying over to New Orleans this afternoon. Some information you can get better on-site."

"Good idea. Do whatever you have to. I have a feeling time is of the essence here."

"I'll do what I can, but you know that this might not have a happy ending."

"I know. I'm hoping for the best."

They finished the conversation, and Bart and the platter of hot, fried seafood made it to the table simultaneously. In spite of everything, he was famished.

He'd thought Jaclyn might be too distraught to have an appetite. Obviously he was wrong. She went for the biggest shrimp, not speaking until the first bite had been chewed and swallowed and her lips licked clean.

"I got the platter for two," she said. "And I ordered extra shrimp. I figured I'd run the bill up high enough so you can have a real moment of Texas pride."

"Nice to be with a woman who cares."

Bart downed a few oysters that he first

dipped in the tangy seafood sauce, then reached for the real delicacy—the soft-shell crab that looked as if it might crawl away if he waited too long to grab it. There was only one. "Want to split this?"

Jaclyn made a face. "I don't eat anything with the arms and legs still attached. It's cannibalistic."

"Those are claws, not arms and legs."

"Still, they're gross."

"Not to another crab." He picked it up and moved it toward her with jerky motions as if it were walking through air. "Eat me, eat me," he cajoled in what he deemed to be a crab voice.

She backed away, truly squeamish. His thoughts took an ugly twist and he imagined her in prison, having her meals from gray metal trays, sitting next to women who'd committed all sorts of vile acts. If a soft-shell crab disturbed her, then prison must have made her physically ill.

He forced the images from his mind—or at least he tried to. They merely skulked to the back corners.

He went back to eating, though even the salty sweetness of the crab that had been fried to perfection lost some of its appeal. Twenty minutes later they were down to a dozen French fries, one crusty slice of garlic French bread and a couple of strips of catfish.

Jaclyn put down her fork and wiped her mouth on the napkin that had been tucked in her lap. "Now that our stomachs are full, I guess the first order of business should be finding a place to stay tonight."

"It shouldn't be difficult to find a hotel room."

"I need a cheap one. I lost my job when I took off to come here, and it's not easy to find a new one when you have to check the ever-been-convicted box."

"What did you do for funds when you left prison?"

"Margo came to the rescue. She showed up when I was released, drove me back to Shreveport and straight to an apartment complex near the university where I'd been an honor student before my arrest. I thought we were visiting a friend of hers. But she'd rented me a place to live, paid the deposit and three months' rent, even had the cupboard and fridge filled with food. That's Margo."

Jaclyn's voice broke and she turned away. "She drove back to New Orleans the next morning. I haven't seen her since."

Bart's composure developed a serious crack in its facade. He suspected at times that he was better with livestock than with people and he knew he was better with horses than with women in tears. Times like this, he usually found a reason to walk away. This time he not only stayed but also pushed the leftovers away and reached for Jaclyn's hands.

"I'm fine," she insisted, but she let her hands stay in his.

"I'll take care of the hotel," he said.

"I'll pay you back."

"We'll worry about that later—when you have a job. Right now I think we should make a visit to Senator Hebert." He paid the bill and filled Jaclyn in on the information he'd gotten from the private investigator as they made the short drive to the senator's New Orleans office.

"Visitor parking is in the lot to the left," Jaclyn said when they bounced over the speed bump at the entrance to the driveway.

"I thought we might peruse the reserved-parking area first." He spotted the car right away, a BMW sedan, top-of-the-line, in a white metallic finish that glistened like diamonds in the afternoon sun. Still, he slowed and checked the license plate. Bingo.

"Senator Hebert is in the house."

STEPPING INTO THE senator's office with Bart by her side seemed only a tad less stressful than it had been when she'd come here alone. But then, she'd expected cooperation from the senator, had imagined that if he didn't know where Margo was he'd be as angst-ridden as she was.

That hope had died quickly and in the process convinced her without a shadow of a doubt that Pat Hebert was behind Margo's disappearance. Why else would he have so vehemently denied knowing her or been so eager to get rid of Jaclyn that he'd practically pushed her out of his office?

The young and very attractive receptionist looked up as they opened the door and stepped inside. The smile quickly turned to a frown when her gaze fixed on Jaclyn. The engraved name block on the front corner of her desk read Brittany Aloysius.

Brittany's attention moved back to Bart. "Can I help you?"

"We're here to see Senator Hebert."

"Do you have an appointment?"

"No," Jaclyn answered. "He's a state senator. I live in the state."

"Senator Hebert is booked for today. If you'd care to make an appointment…"

"Tell him we're here regarding the disappearance of Margo Kite," Bart said, "and that it's urgent we talk to him before we go to the local news channels."

Brittany dropped the pencil she'd been holding and made no attempt to catch it before it rolled off her desk. Bart had definitely caught her off guard. He'd surprised Jaclyn, as well—but pleasantly. For an easygoing cowboy, he definitely knew his way around bureaucratic red tape.

Brittany stood. "I'll be right back."

She left through the side exit that Jaclyn remembered led to the senator's plush office. By the time the door had closed behind her, a door on the opposite side of the room opened and a nice-looking young guy in his early twenties swaggered into the reception area. He looked familiar. When he turned her way, she knew why.

"Win Bronson?"

He broke into a smile. "Jaclyn McGregor. What in the devil are you doing here? Last I heard you were…"

"You can say it. On second thought, don't. It's all behind me."

"Great." He walked over and leaned on Brittany's desk. "So are you back at LSU-S, living in New Orleans, what?"

"I'm planning to start back to school spring semester. And I'm only visiting New Orleans."

"Cool. Maybe we can get together." He gave Bart the once-over. "So what brings you to see Senator Hebert?"

"A problem," she said. "How about you? Why are you here?"

"I'm working for him. He hired me last spring, right after I got my M.A. in poli-sci."

"I'd forgotten you were in political science." And she'd never dreamed he was working for Hebert. This could turn out to be just the break she needed. "I'm in town to visit an old friend," she said. "I don't know if you ever met her. Margo Kite?"

He looked as if she'd just dropped a wiggling scorpion in his mouth, but he recovered quickly. "No. Never heard of her."

"Are you sure? She's a friend of Senator Hebert's, as well. Beautiful young woman, my age, about five-eight. Auburn hair. Nice figure."

"Sounds like my type, but no. I'm sure I've never met her."

And Jaclyn was certain he was lying. She glanced at Bart and knew from his expression that he'd seen the same giveaway look on Win's face when she'd mentioned Margo's name.

Jaclyn introduced the two men. By the time they reached the handshake stage, Brittany had rejoined them.

"The senator will see you now. Follow me, please."

"Good to see you again, Win," Jaclyn said. "Have you got a business card with your cell number on it? Maybe I just will give you a call."

He took a card from his pocket and scribbled his cell number on the back of it. "If I'm out when you call, just leave your number and I'll call you back."

"An old boyfriend?" Bart asked as they followed the vivacious Brittany down the thickly carpeted hallway.

"Yes. Are you jealous?"

"No, you can have him. He's not my type."

His attempt at humor was futile. The familiar dread knotted her stomach. The senator was the key to everything, and if they didn't score any success today, they'd be back to square one. And no matter how hard she tried to hold on to hope, she had the horrifying feeling that time was running out for Margo—if they weren't already too late.

Chapter Seven

Bart judged Senator Patrick Hebert to be in his early fifties, with a few gray strands just beginning to salt his stylish dark brown hair. He was lean, not particularly muscular but toned. Might be a jogger, Bart decided.

He'd run into the senator a few times around Colts Run Cross over the past few years, but they'd never shared more than an exchange of greetings and a comment or two about the weather or ranching. His conclusion was that the senator didn't know more than a comment or two about ranching.

Hebert fit in a lot better here than he did Colts Run Cross. His dark blue pin-striped suit was set off by the pale mauve shirt and darker mauve silk tie, and he sported a Rolex on his left wrist and a diamond-encrusted wedding band on his finger.

He stood when they entered the room, and his smile changed from patronizing to uneasy when his gaze fixed on Bart. Hebert reached across the desk and extended his hand. "Bart Collingsworth, isn't it?"

Bart shook the offered hand. "You have a good memory."

"Most of the time. What brings you to New Orleans?"

"Margo Kite."

The senator turned to Jaclyn. "Margo Kite. That's the friend you were having difficulty getting in touch with, if I remember correctly. Have you located her yet?"

"No."

"I'm sorry to hear that. Won't you have a seat?" He motioned to indicate the two chairs in front of his desk. He sat when they did, assuming the power position behind his massive leather-topped desk. "Now how can I help you?"

The senator was either innocent of any wrongdoing regarding Margo or exceptionally smooth. Bart would reserve judgment as to which until he'd seen and heard more. He scanned the room. A recent photograph of the senator and the woman Bart assumed was his wife stared at him from a silver frame atop a mahogany bookshelf. The woman was attractive in a subdued sort of way, nothing like the youthful hotties Hebert was famed for hitting on in smoky Texas bars.

The senator made a couple of notes on a pad in front of him and leaned forward, locking his gaze with Jaclyn's as if he were keenly interested in what she had to say. "Can you refresh my memory a bit on the situation with your friend?"

Jaclyn bristled noticeably. "Why don't we drop the games, Senator? We both know you were having an affair with Margo before she disappeared without a trace."

"I don't know where you got your information, Miss McGregor, but as I told you before, it's entirely fictional. I'm a happily married man. I don't commit adultery and I won't tolerate such false and destructive accusations. My wife deserves better. Hopefully your friend does, too."

"Were you worried about your wife when

you were telling Margo how you were going to leave your wife for her?"

The senator shook his head as he turned to Bart. "These accusations are totally ludicrous."

"Then you're saying you never met Margo Kite?" Bart asked.

"Not to my knowledge."

"Where have I heard that before?"

"Perhaps I should rephrase that. I meet lots of people in my work. I don't remember all of them. Do you have a photograph of the woman? Sometimes I'm better with faces than names."

"I have the same one I showed you before." Jaclyn opened her handbag and pulled out the picture of Margo that she'd shown Bart on the drive to New Orleans. Leaning forward, she pushed it across the desk toward Hebert.

He picked it up and studied the image, a shot of Margo in white shorts and a bright green halter top, her long auburn hair tossed by the wind. Bart noticed the first fracture in Hebert's armor. A tiny crack but a crack all the same. His eyes gave him away, not with a spark of recognition but with a shadow of pain, as if someone had pricked his skin with a sharp needle. An odd reaction, Bart thought, if he was actually behind Margo's disappearance.

Hebert stood, walked over to Jaclyn and returned the snapshot. "She looks familiar, but I can't place her. Perhaps she worked on one of my campaigns."

"You're lying, Senator." The tone was cold, but the sparks firing from Jaclyn's eyes were searing.

"I don't know what your tie is to Miss McGregor, Bart, but I suggest you try to talk some sense into her. And if she behaves this way with her friends, I can see why they'd move on without telling her how to reach them."

Jaclyn stood and went toe-to-toe, locking horns, so to speak, with the much taller senator. "Margo didn't just move on, and you know that better than anyone."

"That's enough. I want you out of my office now, Miss McGregor."

"I'll go," Jaclyn said, "but this isn't over. I promise you that."

"Are you threatening me?"

"Take it any way you want."

"Fine. Now let me be clear. If you come to this office again, I will have you arrested on the basis of that threat. Not that being arrested will be new for you."

"Go to hell, Senator." Jaclyn walked toward the door.

Bart stood but lingered behind. "How was your trip to Mexico?"

"What's that supposed to mean?"

"I hear you went to Puerto Vallarta the first week in September."

"I was there golfing with some friends—not that I have to explain that to you."

"Margo Kite was on the same flight as you, both going and returning."

"So were a couple hundred other people from the New Orleans area. I don't know most of them either."

"Well, if that's your story…" He turned and followed Jaclyn out of the office.

It wasn't surprising to Bart that Hebert would lie when confronted about an affair with a beautiful woman half his age, especially when the truth could jeopardize his career. Lying did not constitute a felony.

But was he guilty of more? Was he capable of murder?

Bart's gut instinct said no. But he was all cowboy. What the hell did he know about murder?

Which brought yet another question to mind. What was Bart doing here investigating a possible crime with a seductive ex-con whom he barely knew?

No logical answer sprang to mind.

JACLYN'S RED-HOT FURY was fading into the black gloom of desperation by the time Bart signed them into a quaint hotel on a side street in the heart of the Vieux Carré. She hadn't expected Bart to work miracles with Senator Hebert, but she'd hoped that something helpful would come from today's meeting with him.

It hadn't. Margo was still missing, and Jaclyn had no clue what to do next.

"This is the Queen Anne Suite," the hotel manager said as he unlocked the door and pushed it open for Bart's inspection. "It's the largest unit we have. Two rooms with a king bed in the bedroom and a couch that pulls into a bed in the sitting area. And it has a large private courtyard, like you requested."

Jaclyn stepped into the room after the manager and then stopped in her tracks when she saw the decorative black iron bars that covered the street-side windows. The claustrophobic sensation of being locked away hit with crippling force, and her frayed nerves splintered completely. "I can't stay here."

"Don't let those bars worry you," the manager said when she continued to stare at them. "They've been installed on all the first-floor windows as an added security measure, but in fact, we've never had any trouble with crime. You're supersafe here with us."

Bart stepped closer and let his hands rest on her shoulders, steadying and reassuring. "Do you have something on the second or third floors?"

"Yes, but naturally they won't have a courtyard."

"I can do without that. Tight spaces for a night or two won't kill me."

The man frowned. "I don't have any suites upstairs, but I can give you adjoining rooms with small balconies on the street side."

"That will do," Bart said.

Jaclyn's nerves steadied as they followed the manager out of the suite, but now she felt embarrassed by her reaction. The bars were nothing like the ones at the prison, yet the anxiety they'd triggered had been both unexpected and overwhelming. She'd have to work on that.

The manager wasn't nearly as accommodating now that they were taking two regularly priced rooms instead of his fancy suite. They followed him back to the check-in desk, and this time he handed them the keys and sent them on their way.

As it turned out, even the third-floor rooms were French opulent, furnished in antiques, with feather mattress pads and fluffy down comforters in a classy crème de cacao shade.

"What did this cost?" Jaclyn asked.

"In round numbers, six cows and a prize bull."

"You're kidding, right?"

"Don't worry about it. We won't be here long. Once we do the initial groundwork, we can continue the investigation from Jack's Bluff."

She dropped to the bed at that statement, thankful for the soft landing. She hadn't expected Bart to stay away from home this long. This wasn't his battle. But surely he didn't expect her to go back to Texas with him? She worked her feet out of the tennis shoes and pulled them under her on the bed with her as she leaned back on the mound of fluffy pillows.

"Do you want to rest a while?" Bart asked.

She was tired, but sleep seemed selfish, a greedy waste of time that she should be using to search for Margo. "I'm good to go," she said, propping herself up on her elbows. "I'm just not sure *where* to go from here."

"You said you've already been to all the local hangouts and shops and asked if anyone had seen Margo."

"I did that the first few days I was here. I flashed her snapshot all over the Quarter. I ran into several people who said they'd seen her around the area and a few who claimed to know her. None had seen her since I heard from her last or had any idea where she is now."

"Clay Markham is flying to New Orleans today," Bart said. "I imagine that he'll want to talk to you again. How do you feel about meeting him for dinner?"

"Works for me," she said, "though I don't know what else I can tell him."

Bart opened the sliding doors and the breeze ruffled his hair and fluttered the soft white drapery liners. "What do you think about printing and distributing flyers around the area?"

Like *Wanted dead or alive*. The errant thought gave her chills, but she didn't have any better idea. "I don't suppose it could hurt."

"We can print Margo's picture on the flyer and offer some type of reward for information leading to successfully locating her. People who are hesitant to get involved will frequently volunteer information if there's an advantage to their wallet."

Disappointment and frustration set in again. "Not only do I not have money for a reward, but another week without a job and I'll be wearing a sign that says 'Will work for food.'"

"Don't worry about the reward money. It will be my contribution to justice."

The offer touched her—and made her uneasy. She wasn't used to this brand of kindness and generosity. Other than Margo, no one had ever given her anything without expecting more in return.

"I just don't get it. You don't know Margo. You don't know me. Why stick your neck and checkbook on the line?"

He dropped to the bed beside her. "You want the truth—or at least as much of the truth as I know?"

She took a deep breath and exhaled slowly. "I'm not sure, but go ahead."

"You're beautiful, Jaclyn. Sexy. Spunky and vulnerable at the same time. I won't deny that those things play a part in my wanting to help you find Margo. But it's more than that. It is as if fate dropped you into my life because you needed help. Now I feel obligated, even compelled to help you."

"You don't owe me anything, Bart. Fate is a jokester."

"My mother would disagree. She insists that having financial resources entails obligations."

"Noblesse oblige?"

"Right. With wealth and power come responsibilities. That's one of the principles she lives by and tries to make sure we do, as well."

Bart was truly to the manor born. Lucky him, though she couldn't even imagine how that must feel. Her family had consisted of a sperm donor who'd gotten his rocks off one night with Jaclyn's drug-addicted mother. Jaclyn's loving home life had consisted of being verbally abused and physically beaten for something as innocent as walking between her mother and the television set or coming home from school when her mother was with a john.

"I noticed a Kinkos on the way to the hotel," Bart said. "I'm thinking a ten-thousand-dollar reward. I know that's not much as rewards go, but it should be enough to get someone to talk if they know anything. Any more and you bring in the kooks and bounty-hunter types."

Ten grand. She stared at him, too stunned to respond.

"If you don't think that's enough…"

"No," she interrupted before he upped the amount. "That's more than sufficient. You are amazing, Bart Collingsworth." She slipped her arms around his neck, touched her lips to his. She meant the kiss to be quick, just a brush of their mouths. But unfamiliar emotions exploded inside her. Her heart constricted, and she found herself lost in passion and the sweet thrill of his breath mingling with hers.

Finally she pulled away, shaking and struggling for breath.

"Wow!" he exclaimed and held his chest as if he were warding off a heart attack.

"Take it easy, cowboy," she teased, though she felt as if the ground were shaking beneath them. "That was just a thank-you for volunteering the reward."

"Care to go for twenty grand?"

"Don't push your luck."

She knew the kiss was probably a mistake, but the thrill of it lingered as she ducked from his arms and into the bathroom to freshen up. The ecstasy would likely evaporate like mist in the morning sun as soon as they went back to the search and the fears took hold again.

Then again, the kiss might be one of those unexpected pleasures that would warm her heart for a lifetime. But she'd only read about those.

PATRICK HEBERT HAD given up on accomplishing anything at the office after his meeting with Bart Collingsworth and Jaclyn McGregor. He couldn't figure out the bond between Bart and Jaclyn, but it had definitely come at him from out of the blue. He'd figured her for a nobody ex-con who'd give up and go away when no one took her seriously. Bart Collingsworth wouldn't be silenced that easily.

Patrick craved a stiff drink, but if he started with the whiskey this early in the day, he'd end up wasted before dinner. Not that he cared, but his loving wife would.

Candy had made his life a living hell from the first second she'd learned about his involvement with Margo. If he came home drunk, she'd throw it all at him again. And she wouldn't stop with Margo. She'd go back and name every sin he'd ever committed. And there were more than a few.

He wasn't up to her taunts tonight. His nerves were raw as freshly-ground beef, his mind tormented fragments of memories he couldn't shake. The only reprieve he'd found lately was in the drugged slumber he fell into after downing Candy's sleeping pills. But that was hours away.

With no particular destination in mind, he took the ferry to the West Bank, remaining in his car for the short journey across the Mississippi River. The ferry was almost deserted this early in the afternoon, though it would be crowded during the evening rush hour.

Fifteen minutes later, he exited and wound the narrow maze of roads through Algiers. Many of the shotgun-style houses that crowded the area were boarded up, the occupants having never returned after Hurricane Katrina even though this area hadn't been nearly as hard-hit as the ninth ward or the lakefront.

Other homes had been refurbished, their newly painted exteriors shining like beacons among the blighted neglect. His grandfather had once lived a mere block from the levee. The house still stood, on a fashionable block with other old homes that had been preserved and touted as historical landmarks. His grandfather had died a decade ago.

Patrick kept driving, taking the express-

way toward Westwego, though he hadn't
been there since…since Tiffany.

As if on cue, the memories inundated his
mind. Tiffany was not the kind of female a
man could ever forget. She'd been really
young, barely legal. Not that she hadn't
known her way around a bedroom. She'd
pleased him in ways he'd only seen in porn
videos before that. He'd fallen hard.

The way he'd fallen for Margo. No, it was
worse with Margo. She was the kind of
woman who could drive any man mad. She
would haunt his memories forever.

He'd have to make sure that Jaclyn
McGregor didn't.

THE KISS WORRIED BART. Well, not the kiss,
exactly, but the way it had affected him. The
arousal had been instant and almost overwhelming. He'd ached to make love to
Jaclyn right then and there, to simply throw
her across the bed and let his passion and
hunger take over.

He hadn't, of course. For all his feigned
blasé where women were concerned, it was
mostly fright that kept him from forming

emotional attachments with available women. Fear that he'd lose the unfettered cowboy lifestyle that fit him like a pair of favorite jeans.

He'd come close to doing just that a couple of times, and twice was enough to make him constantly wary. He'd been hot and heavy for Amanda Joseph, Houston television's top weather girl, just after graduating from UT. Looking back, he didn't think he'd loved her. But still, she'd practically had him to the altar before the full impact of the situation had hit him.

Marriage to Amanda would have meant following her to wherever a career in television broadcasting took her. He'd figured that wouldn't be within commuting distance to Jack's Bluff. He'd figured right. The last he'd heard, she was a news anchor in San Francisco.

A year after their breakup, he'd fallen for the daughter of the new minister at their church at Colts Run Cross. He'd been pretty sure he was in love that time—or at least well on his way.

He'd proposed marriage. She'd proposed they go to New York on their honeymoon so that she could start applying for a position with one of the big-name advertising agencies. She'd had all of small-town life she could stand. At that point, he'd proposed they call the whole thing off.

He'd dated since then, but he hadn't come anywhere near the commitment stage. But then, he hadn't had a kiss affect him the way Jaclyn's had. He barely knew her, had no real reason to trust her, didn't need her kind of trouble.

Yet there was something about her that just got to him in all the right places and in all the wrong ways. She was a heartbreak waiting to happen, and he preferred his heart remain intact.

Jaclyn tugged him to a stop with her free hand. Her other hand cradled a ream of bright yellow flyers. They were standing in front of a Bourbon Street bar that was already gearing up for the evening. A rock tune was blaring, and a burly hawker stood in the doorway, trying to lure people in with a two-for-one drink offer.

"No drinks," Jaclyn said. "I'm distributing a flyer—"

"No solicitors unless you're drinking," he interrupted.

"In that case, I'm here to see someone."

The guy rolled his eyes and started his spiel on a group of Asian tourists as Bart and Jaclyn maneuvered past him and into the smoky bar. They'd been at the distribution task for over an hour, but they'd hardly made a dent in their stack of flyers. Bart preferred handing them out in person to shopkeepers, bartenders, waitresses, etc. Otherwise, he expected most of them would get thrown into the trash without a second look.

Jaclyn left the flyers with Bart and excused herself to go to the restroom. He straddled a stool at the bar and ordered a cold beer from a young, muscular bartender wearing a black tank top.

"Nice day," the bartender said as he set the bottled brew in front of Bart.

"Lots of sunshine," Bart said.

"Where ya from?" a man two stools down asked.

"I'm from Texas."

"Here on vacation or business?"

"Business." Bart took a swig of the beer, then held up one of the flyers. "I'm offering a ten-thousand-dollar reward for information leading me to this woman." He tapped a finger on Margo's image. "Have you seen her?"

"You must want her bad if you're offering that kind of reward. What'd she do—take your pickup and trailer when she left?" The bartender chuckled at his own humor, finished dispensing a shot of vodka into a tall glass, then leaned over for a look.

The muscles in his face contorted and the veins in his neck stood out. "What's she to you?" he asked, this time with no trace of laughter.

"She's a friend of a friend," Bart answered. "Do you know her?" he asked, though the question was strictly rhetorical. The man's reaction had already proven that he did.

"I know her. And you can tell your friend that her friend Margo is a slut."

"You sound a tad bitter. I take it you two were lovers."

"Something like that."

"How long ago was that?"

"Six months ago."

"What happened to make you break up?" Bart asked.

"I told you—she's a slut. She did what sluts do. She lived with me, drove my car, ran up bills on my credit card, then moved out when something better came along. Same way she left the loser she was dating when I showed up as the new sucker."

"Who was the replacement sucker when she left you?"

"You trying to be funny?"

"No, I'm trying to get information."

"Are you a private investigator or a cop?"

"Neither."

"Sure." He went back to the mixed drink, something with cranberry juice and lime.

"Do you have any idea where Margo Kite is now?" Bart asked.

"Believe me, if I knew, I'd tell you in a New York second. I'd love to get something out of that relationship besides debts and the bad acid trip she took me on. She's probably cleared out of the area by now, before someone gave her what she deserved."

"What would that be?"

"I ain't going there, 'specially not with a cop."

"If you think of anything that might help me locate her, I'd appreciate a phone call," Bart said. "Anything you know or anything you hear. You can call the number on the flyer."

"I'll keep that in mind."

Bart heard Jaclyn's footsteps and decided it might be better to share this info with her without the added interpretive adjectives of the jilted and jaded bartender. It was difficult to put a lot of stake in the word of a man who'd been scorned, but the bartender's opinion of Margo definitely differed from the view of her that Jaclyn had painted. Bart suspected the truth lay somewhere in the middle.

He took another long swig of his beer, then slid off the bar stool before Jaclyn took a seat. "All taken care of," he said, leading her past the laughing group of Asian tourists, who'd taken a table near the door. The street traffic and noise level was steadily picking up as the day grew later, though it was nowhere near as rowdy and packed as Bart remembered it from his Mardi Gras escapade.

Margo slipped one of the flyers from his hand and stuck it on a sandwich sign outside a souvenir store. "I've been thinking about Win," she said.

"Bored with me already?"

"I'll give you a few more hours."

"Talk about pressure."

"I want to see him, Bart—away from the senator's office. He could know something about Hebert's affair with Margo. He might have even seen them together or been with them to the property in Texas. But he'll never admit to knowing anything in front of his boss."

It was a possibility Bart had also considered, but he didn't like where this was going. "I don't think you should see him alone."

She stopped walking and scooted to the edge of the sidewalk nearest the curb, careful not to step into a river of trash that backed up against the concrete. "I just got rid of a warden. I don't need another one."

"You don't need a warden, but you do need protection. Someone came close to killing you two nights ago."

"That wasn't Win!"

"Probably not, but you were quick to

believe it could be the senator, and Win does work for him."

"You don't really think I'd be in danger if I just met Win for a drink?"

He took her hand. "All depends on where you meet. Invite Win to the hotel where we're staying for drinks. Or to any other place you want to meet him where I can stay out of sight but make sure you're safe. Just don't go off alone with him."

Her hand trembled in his. It was almost as if his giving credence to the danger made it more real. "I'm not used to this," she admitted.

"To danger or to having a bodyguard?"

"To having a man worry about me. Scary thing is, it's growing on me."

Scarier yet, it was growing on him, too. And there it was again—an excruciating ache to take her in his arms and never let go.

JACLYN'S CELL PHONE was jangling when she stepped from the shower. She grabbed a towel and ran dripping to catch it before the caller hung up. If it was Win returning her call, she didn't want to miss him. She'd called him before five o'clock, and it was nearly six.

"Hello."

"I saw the flyer." The voice was female, soft, shaky as if the caller was elderly—or nervous.

Jaclyn's hopes shot up. "Do you know Margo?"

"Yes."

"I'm desperate to find her. If you know anything that can help, please tell me."

"She's alone in the blackness. Her spirit cries for you."

The creepiness crawled inside Jaclyn. "Who are you?"

"The messenger. Meet me in front of Jackson Square just after it's fully dark. Come alone."

"How will I recognize you?"

"You won't. I will recognize you." The connection went dead.

The hairs on the back of Jaclyn's neck stood on edge and the towel dropped from her trembling fingers. She stood there in the grayness of the room, the water dripping from her hair and body and soaking the carpet beneath her feet.

Premonitions trickled through her consciousness like ice water being needled into her veins. Whatever the woman had to tell her about Margo, it would not be good.

Chapter Eight

An hour later, Jaclyn stood in the hotel room staring out at the gathering darkness as the old woman's words echoed through her mind. *Alone in the blackness.* For Jaclyn, the words were a nightmarish trip into her own past.

She'd always been horridly afraid of the dark. Her earliest memories were of being left alone at night while her mother roamed the streets looking for her next high. Shivering, she'd cocoon herself in the worn blanket, her heart pounding at every sound, imagining bogeymen under her bed and strangers climbing in through the windows.

That mind-numbing fear had persisted through her teenage years. Even now, she slept with the light on. But tonight the fears were for Margo, hammering the urgency into her brain.

Bart walked in from the balcony, where he'd gone to take a phone call. "That was Clay. His flight was delayed, but he's at his hotel now."

"Does he still want to meet for dinner?"

"Yes. He's discovered some new information he thinks we should know."

"If it's more of the garbage you heard this afternoon, I don't want to hear it."

"He also has a few questions for you."

"Then dinner it is. I should leave soon to meet the caller."

"I don't guess it would do any good to say again that I want to go with you."

"No. She said for me to come alone. I have to honor that. I'll be out in the open with people all around us. I'll be safe."

"And I'll be nearby."

"But out of sight, Bart. You promised. I'm sure she must have seen us this afternoon delivering the flyers. How else could she recognize me?"

"It could be a setup to see what you know."

His unease with the situation added to hers, and the room suddenly felt devoid of oxygen. She walked past Bart and onto the balcony, stepping to the edge and wrapping her hands around the iron railing. Bart followed her.

Her protective cowboy. She was still amazed that he was sticking by her and half expected him to vanish in a poof like the fairy godmother in Cinderella. It was only a matter of time before he came to his senses and escaped back to Jack's Bluff. That was his world, his reality.

"What was it like growing up on the ranch?" The question had slipped from her subconscious to her lips.

He waited so long to answer she thought he might have ignored the question. That would have been fine, too. Hearing about someone else's idyllic childhood would just make her feel worse about her own.

"It was carefree," he said finally. "That's the first word that comes to mind. I don't remember giving it much thought at the time, but I don't think I worried much about anything—until my father died. That was tough, really tough."

"How old were you?"

"Eight. I'd just started third grade. I

wanted to play baseball more than anything back then, but I was lousy. Dad went out back with me every afternoon and helped me practice. After he died, I lost all interest in the sport."

"How did he die?"

"He was a pilot in the National Guard. His copter went down in Texas during a routine training mission. They never discovered the cause."

So Bart's life hadn't been all fun and games. Perhaps no one's had. Maybe the illusion that the rest of the world had pain-free childhoods was a fallacy that lived only in the minds of foster kids.

"It must have been hard on your mother raising a large family alone."

"If it was, she never let on—at least not to us kids. And she wasn't totally alone. She had my grandfather. Jeremiah kind of pinch-hit as a dad and kept the family business going until my brothers and I were old enough to take over some of the responsibilities for Jack's Bluff and Collingsworth Oil."

"I'm sorry I didn't get to meet your grandfather."

"Me, too. Next time. He tires easily these days and is usually asleep by sundown. When he's awake, he mostly just sits and stares at the TV. It's sometimes hard to remember that just a few months ago he was CEO of Collingworth Enterprises and his mental abilities were razor-sharp. But I'm not giving up on him, not by a long shot."

"Is the rest of the family as hopeful of his recovery as you?"

"Yep."

"You and your brothers seem very close."

"We are. We've always spent a lot of time together. We pretty much had to. We didn't have neighbors nearby to play with. But there was no shortage of things to do. Riding, fishing, swimming, roping."

"Roping?"

"Right. I was the best steer roper in the county my senior year in high school. Came in last at state, but that's another story."

"You're lucky," she said. "You probably never felt alone."

"There's different kinds of loneliness, Jaclyn. I saw that with my brother Langston. He seemed to have everything, yet he wasn't really complete until he married the woman he loved."

Bart stepped behind Jaclyn and encircled her waist, letting their fingers meet on the railing. His lips brushed the back of her neck, and her pulse skyrocketed. It would be so easy to fall in love with Bart.

But it would never last. She'd never fit into his world of wealth and family connections, and he'd be a fool to try to make it in hers.

"I should go now, Bart," she whispered. "The woman may be waiting."

"I know."

But instead of letting go of her, he tugged her around to face him. The lights from the street below them danced in his dark eyes, and the clopping sound from a horse-drawn carriage rivaled the pulsing beat of her heart.

Her mind knew to pull away, but the draw was too strong. Her lips met his and the passion erupted in a heartbeat. Their tongues tangled, and his hands twisted in the short locks of her hair. She gave up on fighting the feeling and simply lost herself in the magic of his kiss.

It wasn't until she felt the hardness of his

erection pushing against her that she regained a semblance of control. She placed her hands against his chest and pushed him away, though the burning ache for him refused to let up.

"I know," he said, his voice husky and strained. "You have to go."

She only managed a nod.

"Remember what we talked about," he said. "Stay in the open. She's probably just a resident kook, but play this safe. And don't expect too much."

She nodded again. She knew as well as he did that a woman who simply called herself "the messenger" wasn't the most promising source of information. Yet the frightening premonitions the caller's words had spawned had been so strong that Jaclyn had to believe the woman might know something.

Still, Jaclyn prayed that the blackness she'd spoken of was not a—

No, she wouldn't go there. She'd keep the faith that Margo was alive until she was proven wrong. Hopefully that day would never come.

Hesitant to meet Bart's gaze again and risk falling back into his arms, she walked to the door. He'd be only a few steps behind, watching over her.

She was willing to bet he'd never been afraid of the dark.

WIN LISTENED TO THE message from Jaclyn for the sixth time in the last hour and a half. He'd thought of her far too often since she'd broken up with him after no more than a dozen dates. They'd both been in their freshman year at LSU-S when they'd met. He'd fallen hard, but she'd never been that into him. He'd transferred to the Baton Rouge campus the next semester, and they'd lost touch after that.

What were the odds he'd run into her now under these circumstances? Jaclyn had been serious about her studies, a hard worker who never attended fraternity parties or drank too much. She was the last person he'd have expected to be interested in the disappearance of a party girl like Margo Kite.

But she was, and that made his having anything to do with her risky at best. Yet if he didn't call her back, it might look as if he had something to hide.

Then there was the guy who'd come with her to see Hebert. He had a swagger about him that made Win think he could be a cop— might even be an FBI agent. If he was, then things might already be out of hand.

An eighteen-wheeler sped by him on the right, then swerved into Win's lane. He fired off an offensive gesture and muttered a string of curses. The stress was getting to him.

His cell phone vibrated as a new call came in. Candy Hebert. What the hell did she want now? He'd as soon not know, but she'd only keep calling until he answered.

"Hi, Candy. What's up?" He worked at keeping the irritation out of his voice.

"Pat's not home yet, and Brittany said he left the office mid-afternoon."

"He probably had an appointment away from the office that ran late."

"He's not answering his cell phone."

Smart man.

"I'm worried, Win. The mood he's been in lately, he's likely out drinking. And you know that when he's intoxicated he might say anything."

Babysitting was not in Win's job description—but then, neither were some of the other felonious tasks he'd taken care of lately. "I'll call around and see if I can locate him."

"I appreciate that. Find him and bring him home before he causes trouble for all of us."

"I'll take care of it."

What choice did he have? He was Hebert's new right-hand man, and in politics that meant protecting the boss's image no matter what the man had done.

JACKSON SQUARE WAS A people-watcher's paradise. A mime covered in gold paint entertained a circle of tourists across from the steps to the cathedral. Two teenage boys tapped a few fancy steps on the street, stopping every few minutes to elicit applause and donations from people passing by. A few street artists had their wares displayed along the outside of the fence around the park area.

Jaclyn tried to keep her distance from the others as she scanned the milling groups of tourists. A man who smelled of perspiration and whiskey stopped and asked for money. Another time, she might have given it to him or at least offered to buy him a sandwich. She ignored him tonight, hoping he'd walk away quickly. As he did, a woman approached.

"I'm glad you came," she whispered.

Jaclyn recognized the voice at once. She'd guess the woman to be in her mid to upper seventies, though she could be older. Her shoulders were slightly stooped, and deep wrinkles carved her face into vertical strips.

"How do you know Margo?" Jaclyn asked, afraid that this might have been a hoax call after all.

"She was one of my regular customers, always asking what lay in her future."

Jaclyn's heart constricted. That was Margo, all right, always wanting assurance from what she referred to as "the spirit world." She'd call the psychic hotline before any major decision.

"Are you a fortune teller?"

"I don't particularly like that term. It has bad connotations these days, especially in the Vieux Carré. But, yes, I tell fortunes—among other things."

"What other things?"

"Sometimes I have visions."

"Like a psychic?"

"Yes, I think that better describes me."

"Is that why you call yourself 'the messenger'?"

"One of my early customers started calling me that. It stuck. Margo always called me that. I thought she might have mentioned me to you."

"No, she never did. You said on the phone that Margo was in a blackness, that her spirit was crying out to me. What made you say that?"

"Because it's true, dear. You see, Margo came to see me about three weeks ago. Oddly she didn't want to know her fortune that day. She was sure she already knew it."

"Did she say that?"

"No, but she was glowing, so excited her feet barely seemed to touch the floor. She'd come in to say goodbye. She was leaving town to be with the man she loved."

Chills slithered up Jaclyn's spine. "Did she say where they were going?"

"No, and she didn't mention the man's name, but I knew from past sessions that her lover was married. I never had good vibes about the relationship. At times, she didn't either, but that day she seemed certain that it was going to work out."

"She believed he was going to leave his wife," Jaclyn said. "He didn't. Instead she disappeared. But please tell me what you meant by *the blackness?*"

The woman shuffled and looked around nervously before turning her attention back to Jaclyn. "She hugged me when she left, and as she walked out the door I fell into a trance. The vision was so strong that I lost consciousness for a time. I've had some form of the same vision several times since that day."

The woman's eyes rolled back in her head as if the images were claiming her mind again.

"What is it?" Jaclyn asked. "What do you see?"

"Blood. So much blood." Her voice sounded as if it were being filtered through thick cotton. "It's even trickling down my throat. I'm choking on it, but I can't swallow. I can't move, either, but someone is dragging me. My feet are sliding through the pine straw.

And my head feels as if firecrackers are exploding inside it. Help me. Please help me."

"Tell me how to help you, Margo," Jaclyn pleaded. "Tell me where you are."

The woman started to sway. "It's growing dark. Pitch-black. Everything is black."

Jaclyn grabbed the woman as she stumbled backward. She held her upright as the woman slowly regained her balance and escaped the vision.

"You were in a trance," Jaclyn said. "Were you in touch with Margo? Is she the one who is bleeding?"

"Yes. Someone was dragging her through a wooded area. She was injured and in intense pain."

Anxiety swelled in Jaclyn's chest. "Was that the same vision as you saw the day Margo was leaving?"

"Exactly the same."

"But she wasn't bleeding or in pain then. She was here with you."

"I can't explain the visions. I only have them. But I know that they don't occur in real time. I never know if they're predictions or are things that have already occurred."

"Did you see anything in the vision to indicate where Margo was when she was being dragged through the pine straw?"

The woman squinted and squeezed her face into a wrinkled ball. "There were words, but they were blurry. Three words on a sign. Something about a Cross."

"Colts Run Cross?"

"Possibly."

But Jaclyn was sure that was it. The senator had taken Margo to Texas to get rid of her, the same as he'd planned to do with Jaclyn. He wouldn't have wanted either crime in his home state or anywhere near where he lived and worked.

"I didn't understand why the visions wouldn't let me be," the woman said. "But then I saw you putting out the flyers today, and when I read it I knew you were the one Margo was calling to. I was just the vessel."

"You were great." Jaclyn threw her arms around the woman. "Thank you. Thank you for calling."

The woman drew back. "Perhaps you shouldn't thank me. The blackness is danger, child. Powerful danger. It is always so. You must be very careful or it will ensnare you, too."

"Of course I will be." But adrenaline was shooting through her as she rushed off to find Bart. Caution was the last thing on her mind. Saving Margo was all that mattered.

JACLYN HA. WANTED TO leave for Colts Run Cross immediately. Bart had finally convinced her that it would take a major manhunt to search the property belonging to Hebert and his cohorts. And even if they were already back in Texas and had the search party in place, they couldn't storm private property based on nothing but a vision by a psychic. Nor would law-enforcement officials consider the search urgent without substantial evidence that a crime had occurred.

Instead he'd called his friend Ed Guerra, the sheriff who'd visited her at the hospital just two nights ago. Ed assured Bart that he'd start an immediate investigation, though Ed didn't put much faith in the testimony of a psychic. For that matter, neither had Bart, though he'd unsuccessfully tried to hide his doubt from Jaclyn.

So now she was sitting in Mr. B's Bistro with Bart and Clay Markham, studying the menu and wondering if her jumpy nerves would let her eat.

From listening to Bart describe Clay, she'd expected him to be about Bart's age, but the private investigator was middle-aged, with a receding hairline, a ruddy complexion and a slight paunch around the middle. He was casually dressed in khaki trousers, a striped pullover and a navy sports jacket. She got the impression he was all business, though right now the business seemed to be food.

"Everything's good here," Clay said. "Mr. B's was closed for a quite a while after Katrina hit, but it's back and as great as ever. I try to stop in whenever I'm in New Orleans."

"The blackened redfish is looking good to me," Bart said. "How about you, Jaclyn?"

"Sounds good, unless it's too spicy."

"Their steaks are excellent if you're hungry for beef," Clay said.

The odors and talk of food were getting to her. Maybe she could eat after all. She checked out the steak prices and did a double take. They were probably in line with what a prime steak would cost in any upscale restaurant, but they seemed outlandish to her.

It hit her again how bizarre this whole situation was. Fate must have been drunk when it hooked a woman like her up with wealthy rancher Bart Collingsworth.

The waiter returned and filled their glasses with the deep burgundy Cabernet Bart had selected from the extensive wine list. For a man who claimed to spend most of his hours around cows, he certainly knew his way around Napa and Sonoma varieties.

She decided on the filet mignon with a side salad and an order of steamed asparagus. She might never get the chance to dine so magnificently again. But her appetite vanished the second the waiter walked from earshot and the real purpose for the dinner meeting got under way.

"How much do you know about Margo's problems in Dallas?" Clay asked.

"I don't remember any problems. She broke up with her boyfriend, got bored and decided to move to New Orleans. That's how she was. When she got bored she'd move on. I explained that this morning."

"It was a little more involved than that," Clay said. "From what I could learn so far, she was arrested for stealing some valuable paintings from the house of a man she'd been living with."

"There must be some mistake," Jaclyn said. "True, I was incarcerated at the time, but she would have told me if she'd been arrested."

"Maybe she didn't want to worry you."

Jaclyn turned the stem of her glass and stared at the swirling liquid. "If there was a problem, the police must have realized she was innocent and released her."

"The paintings showed up on the black market, and the owner regained possession. He dropped charges."

"He probably gave them to her and then changed his mind when she left him. Men are like that around Margo. They fall all over themselves doing things for her."

"Interesting." Clay scribbled a few lines in a small black notebook. "Tell me more about her."

"I told you what I know over the phone this morning."

"You gave me facts. Tell me how you became so close."

"We met under miserable circumstances, as foster siblings in a home where we were treated like servants and constantly subjected to humiliation. She always stood up for me even when it got her in trouble."

"How long were you in the same home?"

"Six months, during our sophomore year in high school. Margo hated all the rules and wearing nothing but hand-me-down clothes. She decided to run away. She begged me to go with her, but I was afraid to. And I was determined to stay in school, keep up my grades and get a scholarship."

"Did you see her after she ran away?"

"Not often. She left town, but she'd find a way to call at least once a week. In between, she'd send me e-mail messages from an Internet café. I'd go to the public library near where I was living and read and answer them."

"So there was never a time when she just went off and didn't keep in touch?"

"Never!"

"And you didn't have an argument before she quit corresponding three weeks ago?"

"No. We both have cell phones now, so we pretty much talked or text-messaged each other every day."

"Then I can definitely understand why you're so certain she's in some kind of trouble."

That response won him brownie points and made Jaclyn significantly more cooperative for the rest of the question-and-answer session. They talked through the salad course, but when the entrées were served, Clay's interest turned to a porterhouse steak that spilled over the edges of a generous platter.

In spite of her fears, Jaclyn ate ravenously. It was likely the best steak she'd ever eaten. Still, by the time they'd finished and were sipping after-dinner coffee, her mood had darkened again and her mind was back on the psychic's vision.

Clay fingered the handle of his coffee cup. "I have more news. I didn't want to ruin Jaclyn's dinner, but I don't think I should put it off any longer."

Jaclyn stiffened, dreading what might come next.

"It seems that Margo Kite is not the first of Senator Hebert's female love interests to disappear. Seven years ago, the same thing happened to an eighteen-year-old named Tiffany Sparks. Her ex-boyfriend—a guy named Colin Green—claimed she was having an affair with Pat Hebert, though he wasn't a senator at the time. Attorney Pat Hebert denied knowing her."

Just as he'd done with Margo. "Was Tiffany ever found?" Jaclyn asked.

"Yeah. One month later. But…"

He hesitated, and the silence grew deafening as they waited to hear the rest.

Chapter Nine

Clay Markham propped his elbows on the table and worried an opened package of sweetener, not noticing as the contents spilled onto the linen tablecloth. "Tiffany's body was found in a wooded area in Marrero. That's on the West Bank, about twenty miles from downtown New Orleans. She'd been shot twice in the head and buried in a shallow grave. The body washed up in a heavy rain, and a man found it while walking his dog."

Chills slithered up Jaclyn's spine as the grotesque images took shape in her mind. "Did they suspect that Pat Hebert killed her?"

"No. They thought it was the ex-boyfriend from the get-go. Tiffany's parents reported that Colin had been stalking her since the breakup and calling her at all hours of the day and night. They insisted she wasn't seeing anyone else at the time and that Colin had made up the affair with Pat Hebert to get himself off the hook."

"Why would he have picked Pat Hebert?" Bart asked.

"Hebert was running for councilman at the time and there had been a couple of articles about him in the *Times-Picayune*. The lead detective in the case noted Colin could have pulled the name out of a hat in a moment of panic."

"Sounds like a long shot," Bart said.

Jaclyn took another sip of the strong coffee, but it did nothing to melt the icy trembles inside her. "What happened with the boyfriend?"

"He rode his motorbike off an elevated Westbank Expressway exit one morning about two o'clock. He died instantly. There were no witnesses to the accident."

Which meant he could have been run off the road, the same way she'd been run off when leaving Colts Run Cross.

Bart leaned in closer. "So no one was ever arrested for the murder?"

"No, it's still an open case, but apparently the cops were so sure the ex-boyfriend was guilty they shifted it to the back burner. It's in the cold-case files."

The similarities between Tiffany and Margo were more than bizarre. Tiffany had been eighteen. Margo was twenty-three. But then, the senator was seven years older now than at the time of the first disappearance.

Tiffany had been murdered. Shot in the head. Dragged bleeding into a wooded area—the same as Margo had been in the psychic's vision. Jaclyn started to shake. She had been fighting the thought that Margo might be dead, but now the possibility wouldn't let go of her and she was feeling sick. "If there's nothing else, I'd like to go back to the hotel," she said.

Bart reached over and squeezed her hand, but this time his touch did nothing toward alleviating the anxiety.

"That's it for now," Clay said. "I'll get back to you as soon as I learn anything new. How long do you plan to stay in New Orleans?"

"We're heading back to Jack's Bluff in the

morning," Bart answered. "I think I mentioned to you that Hebert and some of his friends own property near Colts Run Cross. They come out there to play cowboy—and I'm sure it gives them a tax write-off."

"And you think Hebert may have taken Margo there?"

"Actually, I may as well tell you the whole story."

Jaclyn listened as Bart explained the psychic's vision. Clay didn't openly scoff, but it was clear he put little faith in the information in spite of the similarities between the psychic's image and his explanation of Tiffany's murder.

When they finally left the restaurant, Jaclyn took huge gulps of the cool night air. Slowly the nausea passed, though the apprehension continued to swell. "Can we walk a while?" she said.

"We can do anything you want." He took hold of her hand and strode beside her, past shops and street musicians and horse-drawn carriages, not stopping until they reached the river.

A large cruise ship was docked nearby, its

lights as bright and as numerous as a small city. The odors of beer and frying beignets wafted on the air along with a haunting trumpet solo about love gone wrong.

Jaclyn was beginning to understand how Margo had ended up in this city. It was edgy, restless, as she was, always looking for something to hold her interest and excite her. And she'd ended up in the arms of Senator Patrick Hebert.

Her cell phone rang, startling her. She checked the caller ID. "It's Win. Should I take it?"

"That's up to you," Bart said, "but remember what we talked about. Don't see him anywhere that's not completely public and in the open, preferably the small bar in our hotel."

Her finger slipped as she pushed the talk button and for a second she thought she might have dropped the call. "Win?"

"Yeah, it's me. Sorry to be so late getting back to you, but I had a meeting tonight."

"That's okay. It's just that I'm leaving town tomorrow and I'd hoped we could get together."

There was a pause. Finally he said, "I didn't realize you were leaving so soon."

"I had a change of plans."

"Sorry to hear that. We could have had some fun."

But she could hear the relief in his voice.

"Are you going back to Shreveport?"

"Yes," she said, the lie coming easier than she would have anticipated. Better he not know she was going to Colts Run Cross.

"I know it's late," Win said, "but New Orleans doesn't come alive until midnight. I can pick you up at your hotel and we can go to Pat O'Brien's for a drink. It's a must-do on every tourist's list."

"I turn into a pumpkin at midnight, but I can probably make it through one drink. How about we have it at my hotel? There's a lovely bar and it's quiet enough we can talk and catch up on old times. You can do your Professor Hastings impersonation."

"God, I haven't thought about him in forever. Okay. Where are you staying?"

She didn't talk about Margo or Tiffany on the walk back to the hotel. Putting terrifying possibilities into words wouldn't help her make it through the approaching rendezvous with Win Bronson.

BART WAS MORE UNEASY than ever after the meeting with Clay. A lot had happened since they'd arrived in New Orleans at noon today. Too much, and his body and mind felt the impact.

And as much as he hated to give credence to the visions of a proclaimed psychic, there was no denying that the situation she described for Margo closely paralleled what had actually happened to Tiffany Sparks.

He watched as Jaclyn glossed her lips and smoothed her bangs, pushing them to the side. "Planning to try seducing the old boyfriend?" he teased, though his heart wasn't in it.

"Unless he's changed since I knew him, seducing him is not a challenge. I just hate to have him think I've aged more than he has. It's a woman thing."

"Not necessarily."

She brushed on fresh mascara. "Now that I've agreed to meet him for a drink, I'm having difficulty remembering what I thought I could gain by talking to him."

"Maybe he'll slip up and admit that the senator and Margo were an item."

"Or that Hebert took Margo vacationing in Mexico," she added. "But it could be that he was telling the truth and has never met Margo. The senator may keep his indiscretions a secret from staff members."

"Could well be. Just remember the rule— don't leave the bar with him. And call if you need me."

He stepped behind her and caught a wisp of her perfume. It was light and flowery, like spring at the ranch. He trailed his fingers down her arms and grew heady with awareness.

He ached to hold her in his arms. Hungered for another taste of her lips. Was crazy to make love to her.

There. He'd admitted it. And now that the thought was in his head, he'd have a devil of a time getting free of it, especially when she'd be sleeping a mere door away.

She checked her watch. "It's time. Wish me luck?"

"You know it."

And then Jaclyn was gone, off to meet an

old boyfriend with ties to a man who might be behind the attempt on her life two nights ago.

Bart gave her time to reach the bar before taking the staircase to the first floor and the back entrance to the courtyard. Moving among the shadows, he picked a spot away from the illumination and beneath a cluster of banana trees.

Someone else had occupied the spot before him and conveniently left one of the padded deck chairs along with a scatter of cigarette butts. He spotted Win and Jaclyn a minute later, taking a settee near a fake fireplace. He was fairly certain they couldn't see him in the dark, but he had a great view of them.

Win snaked his arm along the back of the settee and whispered something in Jaclyn's ear that made her smile. An unwelcome pang of jealousy tightened his chest. He ignored it. Win was the past. Bart was the here and now. And tomorrow Jaclyn would be going home with him to Jack's Bluff.

He'd figure out his feelings for her on his home turf, where he knew who he was and what he was about. Right now the focus had to be on finding Margo and keeping Jaclyn safe.

And making it through the night without jumping Jaclyn's bones.

"TELL ME ABOUT YOUR job," Jaclyn said as Win finished his beer and ordered a second. She'd barely touched her after-dinner liqueur. So far, the talk had centered on old times, an obligatory topic which probably held as little interest for him as it had her.

"The job is great. Senator Hebert's on the cutting edge of the rebuilding of New Orleans. He's a mover and shaker in the state senate, too. I'm in on a lot of the action. He refers to me as his assistant, but basically I'm an idea man. He runs almost everything by me and even includes me in family activities."

"Does he have children?"

"No, but his wife has two brothers, one a judge and the other the area's top criminal defense attorney. They're definitely part of the happening scene."

"Sounds fascinating. Did you go to work for Senator Hebert right out of college?"

"Yeah. How's that for starting at the top?"

"You must have made some impression at your interview."

Win smiled flirtatiously at the cute young waitress who appeared with the beer. He watched her walk away before turning his attention back to Jaclyn. "Actually, Pat's wife had a lot to do with him hiring me. Candy liked my ideas and thought her husband needed a youthful male on his team."

As opposed to the youthful woman he was sleeping with, Jaclyn guessed. She'd left several messages on the Heberts' home phone when she'd first arrived in New Orleans and even made a visit to the senator's home. Someone had returned her phone. Calls with the message that Candy Hebert was in France to attend a seminar and enjoy an extended vacation. She'd been told the same by the housekeeper when she'd tried to push her way into the Hebert home.

"What's his wife like?"

"Good-looking for her age."

"Which is?"

"Candy's mid-forties, I think. She's active

in politics, mostly backing Pat, but she has a mind of her own. They have a great marriage."

Jaclyn studied Win, wondering if he really believed that or if this was more of his PR routine. She couldn't tell. "Your boss had an affair with my friend Margo Kite."

Win wrapped his hand around his beer bottle but didn't lift it. "Pat told me why you came to see him. I don't know where you got that idea, but it's crazy."

"Do you really believe that your boss isn't capable of sleeping around?"

"I'm not saying he's never tempted. Pat appreciates a good-looking woman just like the rest of us, but he doesn't run around on his wife."

"Maybe you don't know him as well as you think you do."

"I was thinking the same about your friend. If she's the kind who brags about having an affair with a married man, what makes you think she wouldn't lie about his identity?"

"Why would she?"

"You tell me. Maybe she just wanted to entertain you with a good story while you were stuck behind bars."

Leave it to Win to bring that up.

"Look, Jaclyn, I can see why you're worried about your friend, but wasting your time harassing the senator won't help you find her. If anything, it's distracting you and keeping you from finding out what really happened."

Win delivered the spiel flawlessly. She wasn't buying. Reaching into the side pocket of her handbag, she pulled out the snapshot of Margo and thrust it in front of him. "Are you sure you've never seen this woman with the senator?"

Win studied the photo, smirking as he returned it. "Believe me, if I'd seen this woman, I'd remember her. I'd have probably hit on her myself. Pat Hebert wouldn't have."

She didn't know if he was telling the truth, but it was clear she wouldn't get any helpful information from him. She stretched and rubbed the tendons in her neck, suddenly feeling stress in every muscle of her body.

"I guess we'll have to agree to disagree on the senator," she said. "It was nice talking with you, but…"

Unexpectedly Win dropped his arm from around her shoulders and took her hand.

"You need to let this go, Jaclyn." His voice took on a serious edge. "Your friend lied and now she's probably run off with a loser and just doesn't want to tell you."

Ire coursed through her veins. "You don't know Margo, so don't call her a loser. She was having an affair with Senator Hebert, and he's behind her disappearance. I'm not giving up until I prove it."

He dropped her hand and stared at her as if she'd dropped in from Mars. "Do you really think the police or anyone else in authority will put the word of someone with a criminal record over Senator Hebert's? Face it, Jaclyn. You're an ex-con and your friend is a slut who brags about sleeping with married men. Nobody will care what you say or where she ran off to."

That did it. Jaclyn picked up the glass and tossed the rest of her drink into his face. Her only regret as she stormed out of the bar was that the senator wasn't there so she could toss one in his face, too.

EXHAUSTED, BART HAD fallen asleep within minutes after his head hit the pillow. He'd slept solidly—for three hours. Now he was lying awake and staring at the shadows that sneaked into the dark corners of his room and slinked across the ceiling.

He smiled thinking of Jaclyn dousing Win with her drink. The look on the pompous jerk's face had been priceless. And after Jaclyn had told him what Win had said to prompt her action, he had to admit that the guy had it coming.

Jaclyn had spunk. But then, Bart had known that from the moment he'd pulled her out of the wreck. Still, she was being pushed to her limits, and there seemed to be no letup of bad news.

Tiffany Sparks, young and probably innocent. Murdered and buried in the woods as if her life hadn't mattered at all. It would take some kind of deranged bastard to commit an act like that. But the daily news was proof that the world was full of deranged bastards.

But was Patrick Hebert perverse and unhinged enough to kill a young woman or have her killed in order to save his political hide? Not once but twice—or maybe more? The prospect was chilling and opened possibilities almost too horrifying to imagine.

And if he'd murdered Margo, he wouldn't hesitate to kill Jaclyn, the one person determined to find the truth. Bart's chest constricted and he felt as if a rope were tightening around his ribs and pushing them into his heart. He couldn't let anything happen to her. He wouldn't.

His brothers would never understand how he'd become so emotionally entangled with her in such a short time. Hell, he didn't understand it himself. He rolled over and then tensed at the sound of footsteps in the hall outside his door. Late-night partyers, he guessed. But then, in the filtered glow of the moonlight, he saw his doorknob turn. Someone was breaking into his room.

He jumped up and positioned himself so that he'd be behind the door and ready for a surprise attack when it opened. But the knob quit turning and the footsteps moved on. Just someone at the wrong door. But the adrenaline was pumping fast and furious through Bart's veins now.

This time it had been a mistake. Next time it might not be. He tiptoed to the door that separated him from Jaclyn and eased it open so that he could assure himself she was sleeping safely. The covers were pushed to the foot of the bed. The bed was empty.

His heart slammed into his chest…before he spotted Jaclyn curled up in the chair next to the window with her head resting on her arms. He stood there, mesmerized by how sweetly beguiling she looked when she was asleep.

She stirred, opened her eyes and lifted her head. "Bart?"

"Yeah. It's me. I heard some noise in the hall. It was nothing, but I wanted to check on you."

She stretched and pushed her feet back to the floor. "I couldn't sleep. I kept thinking about the physic and about the blackness."

"I couldn't sleep either," he said.

"Then stay with me, Bart. Sleep in my room. I don't want to be alone."

His breath caught in his throat. How could he say no to that?

Chapter Ten

The drapes were pushed back, and moonlight streamed into the room. Jaclyn was near the window, curled in the large armchair and draped in the hotel blanket. She looked ethereal in the silvery glow, and Bart stared, mesmerized, as arousal tensed every muscle.

He ached to pick her up, carry her to the bed and crawl in beside her, wanted her with an intensity that bordered on ludicrous considering the circumstances. And yet...

He took a deep breath to give his few functioning brain cells a chance to check in. He wanted her, but not like this. When he made love to Jaclyn, he wanted it to be more than her seeking comfort from a warm body.

He took a seat on the wide windowsill.

"You've had a rough few hours, Jaclyn, no wonder you're too keyed up to sleep."

"More morose than keyed up," she said. "I keep thinking about what the psychic said about the darkness. And what the private investigator said about Tiffany Sparks."

"The evidence against Senator Hebert is purely circumstantial," he said, hoping to ease her fears though his own had grown exponentially since their meeting with Clay. "There's no concrete evidence Hebert even knew Tiffany Sparks. And the cops must have had valid reasons for believing the ex-boyfriend killed Tiffany or they wouldn't have just let the murder case grow cold."

"Cops make mistakes. They did with me. So did a judge and jury."

His muscles flexed painfully as the disturbing image of her behind bars slunk back into his mind. "You have a reason to be bitter about that. I can't even imagine how hard being falsely imprisoned must have been."

She pulled her feet back up to the chair with her and hugged her knees to her chest. "It wasn't that different than the rest of my life had been."

He hadn't wanted to bring up anything that would add to her sadness, but now that she'd brought it up, he felt he should ask. "You told Clay you met Margo in a foster home. What happened to your parents?"

"I never knew who my father was. My mother died of a drug overdose when I was twelve," she said, a haunting sadness settling into her voice. "But she wasn't really a mother. I never remember her cooking a meal or tucking me in at night. Most nights she wasn't even there. My earliest memories are of being scared and alone."

Bart ached for her and tried to imagine growing up without his mother. He couldn't. His earliest memories were of family and of being loved.

Jaclyn hugged the blanket around her. "The part that haunts me most about being in prison is the clanging slam of that iron door when it closed behind me on that first night. I still wake up in a cold sweat lots of nights with that devastating echo ringing in my ears."

Bart left the window and walked the few feet to her chair, settling on the arm of it. Her nearness seeped into his senses like a drug, making it hard to swallow, harder to think. "Did you have that dream tonight?"

"No, tonight's horror was new. I was trying to pull Margo out of a pitch-black hole, but she was stronger and she was pulling me in with her."

She shuddered and he pulled her close. "It was just a nightmare."

"Was it, Bart? Because I'm awake now, and it's not fading away, no more than my past is. It's exactly like Win said. Who'll believe the word of an ex-con over a prominent politician? And my ex-con status will never go away."

"You can clear your name, Jaclyn. All you have to do is prove your innocence. I know this attorney in Houston named Phil Caruthers, and my—"

She put two fingers over his lips. "Don't, Bart. Please don't dangle Collingsworth-type options in front of me."

"I was trying to help."

"The only help I need from you is in finding out what happened to Margo."

The change in her wording caught him off guard. Before tonight it had always been *find*

Margo—now it was find out what had happened to Margo. She was obviously beginning to accept the fact that they might not find Margo—and that if they did, she might not be alive.

No wonder she'd been curled up in what was practically a fetal position when he'd walked in. He slid into the chair with her and lifted her onto his lap, cradling her in his arms. His body reacted instantly, but he forced the urges into submission. No matter what she'd said earlier, no matter what he wanted, what Jaclyn needed tonight was a friend.

She cuddled against him. In minutes he heard the soft rhythmic sound of her breathing and knew she'd fallen back asleep. He held her until the clatter of garbage cans in the street below them signaled the dawn of a new day before carrying her back to bed.

She needed her rest. He probably did, too, but he had too much on his mind now. Still, he stood there for another minute, watching her sleep.

Damn! He had it bad. He wondered how long it would take his brothers to figure that out. With Langston, probably five minutes tops.

Still, Bart couldn't wait to get back to Jack's Bluff. He was a rancher. He just plain thought better around green pastures and cows than he did surrounded by pollution and concrete.

IT WAS NINE O'CLOCK. and they'd been on the road an hour when Aidan Jefferies returned Bart's phone call. Bart explained the situation and his concern over whether or not Ed Guerra could get a warrant and search Paradise Pastures Ranch.

"If you want this to go down quickly, you need something more concrete to give the judge than suspicion," Aidan said.

"Like what?"

"Evidence that Margo Kite was either with Senator Hebert in Texas or on the ranch the last time she was seen. What's the chance you can get that?"

"Only chance of that would be getting the ranch foreman or someone who saw them together in Texas to cough up the info."

"Do you know the foreman?"

"Not well. He's not from around here and not the friendliest of guys. He's never exchanged more than a few words when I've run into him around Colts Run Cross. But then, Paradise Pastures barely has enough livestock to qualify as a ranch."

"What's the foreman's name?"

"Rene Clark."

"Have you had him checked out?"

"I've got a private investigator on him as of about an hour ago."

"Good move. I'll run a criminal check on Clark, too. Something might turn up that will give you the edge with him. In the meantime, don't do anything rash, Bart. You have to play this cool. Get off on the wrong foot and it can backfire."

"Okay, as long as the right foot doesn't take too long to step into action. I'd like to talk to Rene no later than tomorrow morning."

"You really believe this Jaclyn McGregor is leveling with you, don't you?"

"Yeah. I know that might sound naive on my part."

"You said it, not me."

Bart was well aware how his belief in

Jaclyn would look to everyone else, yet he did believe her. "I have to go with my gut feeling on this," he said.

"Then I'll see what I can find out."

"Thanks."

"Have you talked to Langston about this?"

"Some. I'm not keeping secrets, if that's what you're thinking."

"I just didn't want to go say anything to him if you hadn't. I don't like going behind another man's back."

"You won't be. Thanks for the help, Aidan."

He broke the connection and explained the gist of the phone conversation to Jaclyn. By the time he finished, his cell phone was ringing. It was Langston. Obviously Aidan had wasted no time in calling him, probably to tell him that Bart was sliding off the deep end.

"Good morning, Langston."

"I just talked to Aidan."

"Somehow I was certain you had. I'm not in the mood for lectures."

"Good. I don't have time to waste on them. When are we going to talk to Rene Clark? You know, I always kind of figured him as a snake in the grass. It will be fun to see him squirm."

"Tomorrow morning, after I talk to the sheriff, but you don't have to go along."

"Why would I want to miss the fun? Besides, isn't All for One and One for All the Collingsworth motto?"

"I think that was the Three Musketeers."

"Those rats. They must have stolen it from us."

"Since you're going to be involved, Langston, would you mind explaining the situation to Mom and telling her that Jaclyn will be staying with me in my house for a few days?"

"You're bringing Jaclyn back to Jack's Bluff?"

"Yeah. Do you have a problem with that?"

"I just wonder if it's the best move under the circumstances."

The circumstances being that she was an ex-con who'd been released from prison only a few weeks ago. Langston hadn't said it, but Bart knew what he was thinking. Bart might have thought the same thing if he hadn't spent the last twenty-four hours with her.

"The circumstances are that she's safer with me," Bart said.

"I'm just surprised, that's all. I'll talk to Mom."

"Was that more bad news?" Jaclyn asked once he'd broken the connection.

Bart kept his eyes on the road, but he reached across the seat and took her left hand in his right one. "Good news," he said, trying to paint an encouraging picture for her sake. "My brother Langston wants to go with me to talk to Hebert's foreman. He's a great negotiator. If anyone can get the guy to talk, it will be Langston."

"Do you think we need him?"

"We?"

"You surely didn't think I was going to stay back at the ranch while you questioned someone about Margo?"

He definitely hadn't planned on taking her along. "If the senator was behind having you run off the road the other night, then he's probably already warned the foreman not to talk to you."

"If the senator is behind my being run off the road, I'm sure he's told the foreman not to talk to anyone about Margo. I'm going with you, Bart, and that's that."

Bart dropped the subject. As their neighbor Billy Mack would say, a man has to have an IQ the size of his boots to argue with a stubborn woman. Bart prided himself on being a smart man.

LANGSTON LOVED IT when Trish dropped by the office unexpectedly, though he knew she was here to have lunch with his mother today instead of to visit with him. There were still days he could barely believe that he'd found her and the daughter he hadn't known existed again after sixteen years. It might be possible to be happier than he was now, but he didn't see how.

He met her at the door and gave her a long, slow kiss. "You look terrific, Mrs. Collingsworth."

"Thank you, Mr. Collingsworth. There's this man I'm trying to impress."

"It had better be me." He held her close, then released her reluctantly. "Where are you and Mother going for lunch?"

"Brennan's. For the turtle soup. I've been craving it all week. Then we're planning to stop by the Galleria for an hour or so to do some shopping. What time do you want to leave for the ranch?"

"There might be a little problem there."

Trish dropped into one of the chairs. "What kind of problem?"

He propped his backside against his desk, facing her. They had spent the biggest part of the past four weekends at the ranch. Their daughter Gina was working on perfecting her barrel-racing skills for the spring rodeo competition. She was getting really good. Langston was just thrilled that both his daughter and his wife loved the family ranch the way he did.

"So give," Trish prompted. "What's the problem?"

"Bart's bringing the woman he rescued the other night back to the ranch."

"Have they already found her missing friend?"

"No, but the investigation has led them back to Colts Run Cross." He'd just started to explain the situation when his secretary buzzed him that his mother was there to meet Trish. He had Lynette show her in.

"I'm just catching Trish up on the latest with Bart," he said after the greetings were finished.

"You heard from him?"

"This morning. He's on his way back to the ranch."

"Great. That must mean he found Jaclyn's friend. Was she okay?"

"They haven't found her, but they think there's a chance Margo Kite might have been a guest at Paradise Pastures before she disappeared."

"What makes them think that?"

Langston explained the situation with Patrick Hebert and the Paradise Pastures Ranch as best he could, right down to the psychic's vision. "I don't put any faith in psychic visions," Langston added.

"I do," Trish said. "And hearing about that vision gives me chills. Suppose the senator did kill Margo to keep her quiet about their affair and then buried her body on the ranch?"

"We don't even know for certain there *was* an affair," Langston reminded her. "And if there was, killing her was the least plausible likelihood."

"Then why hasn't she gotten in touch with Jaclyn?" Trish asked.

"Maybe he paid her off and she took the money and left the country."

"You can read and send e-mails from out of the country," Lenora said.

"I feel so sorry for Jaclyn," Trish said. "I pray Margo is okay. It's so hard to lose a friend, especially to a killer."

No one knew that any better than Trish. She'd lost her best friend to a killer just months before.

Lenora walked to the huge plate-glass window and stared out at the view of downtown Houston. It was rather spectacular from the eighteenth floor, but from the troubled look on his mother's face, he knew she wasn't appreciating the vista today.

Finally Lenora turned back to Bart and Trish. "If the national news media gets wind of this, they'll be all over the story. Senator Hebert won't be able to intimidate them. That may be the fastest route to a warrant."

"But then Jaclyn's past would come out as well," Trish said. "And then who will believe her?"

Lenora spun around. "What past?"

"I was about to get to that," Langston said.

He'd told Trish the truth from the beginning, but it hadn't seemed necessary to tell his mother—until now. "Jaclyn was convicted of stealing money from her employer, though she insists she was set up. She was released just over a month ago. Margo picked her up from prison, gave her some money to live on until she could get a job and set her up in an apartment. That's when she told her that she and the senator were in love and he was going to leave his wife for her."

Lenora ran her fingers through her short, graying hair, then smoothed the front of her suit jacket. "Why didn't Bart mention that the other night?"

"He didn't know it the other night," Langston said. "Aidan Jefferies found out about her police record. She admitted everything after that—not that she had much choice in the matter. And, for the record, her name is Jaclyn McGregor, not Jaclyn Jones."

"I just hope Bart knows what he's doing," Lenora said.

"Bart's a smart man," Langston said, "with good instincts. But you should also know that Jaclyn isn't married to a fighting serviceman or to anyone else. She said it was a ruse to keep men from hitting on her."

Lenora frowned. "I can see how that could be a problem for her. She's beautiful. But that changes things a bit, doesn't it?"

"Are you uneasy with having Jaclyn at the ranch?" Trish asked.

"A little," Lenora admitted, "but not because I think she's dangerous. In fact, I liked her when I met her—and I have good instincts, too. It's Patrick Hebert who worries me."

Langston put a hand on his mother's shoulder. "Under the circumstances, I don't think you need to worry about him. He might have tried to frighten off Jaclyn, but he's not crazy enough to take on the whole Collingsworth clan. I expect he's staying close to home and keeping a low profile now."

"Then why suggest that Gina and I not go to the ranch?" Trish asked.

"I just thought you might not want to get involved," Langston said.

"I'm part of the family. Why wouldn't I be involved? And Gina's counting on it."

"Fine," Langston said. "I'll pick you and

Gina up right after she gets in from school. So count us in for the weekend, Mom."

"Good. I think we all have to stand behind Bart in this. He's trying to do the right thing."

Or else he was being jerked around by a pro with her own agenda. As far as Langston was concerned, the verdict was still out on that.

BART HAD TRIED TO prepare Jaclyn for Friday-night dinner at Jack's Bluff, but his description of the boisterous camaraderie and enormous quantities of fabulous foods hadn't even come close to capturing the true atmosphere.

The entire family was present, including Jeremiah, who sat at one end of the massive oak table while Bart's mother occupied the chair at the other end. Jeremiah uttered only a few short sentences but managed to contribute greatly to the havoc by banging his cane on the floor whenever he wanted someone to refill his glass with iced tea or to pass a food item his way.

Jaunita bustled back and forth from the kitchen carrying huge platters of pork chops, biscuits and homemade tortillas, along with bowls of green beans, sweet potato casserole and stuffed poblano chilies. The plump cook chatted while she served, not only remaining unperturbed by the men's teasing, but hurling it right back at them.

And the family members, all twelve of them, chatted, laughed and kidded each other as if they were the best of friends. It was easily the most amazing display of family affection and harmony Jaclyn had ever seen. The scenario made her feel miserably out of place and painfully guilty for imposing on them with her presence and problems.

"Did you get enough to eat?" Bart asked as he forked his last bite of sweet potatoes.

"Too much, but everything was delicious."

Jeremiah hammered his cane against the floor as he'd done frequently during the meal when he wanted attention. Not that he couldn't speak. He had uttered a short sentence from time to time, but the syntax got mixed up, and the ordeal of talking seemed frustrating for him.

"Are you ready to go back to your room?" Lenora asked, seemingly understanding what Jeremiah wanted even without words.

He nodded.

"Let me take him," Trish offered.

Jeremiah shook his head.

"Thanks for the offer," Lenora said, "but he gets upset if anyone but me helps with the after-dinner bedtime rituals." She stood as Bart helped Jeremiah to his feet.

"There's *tres leches* for dessert," Jaunita announced as she gathered empty dishes. "Is anyone ready?"

"Let's wait for Mom to get back," Becky suggested.

"Great idea," Trish agreed. She stood and started to help Jaunita with clearing the table. "Jaime, let's take over the cleanup chores for Juanita so she can go home and have dinner with her family."

"That's not necessary," Juanita said. "I can finish up these dishes in *uno momento*."

"So can we," Becky insisted. "So scoot."

"You make me to get *perezoso*," Juanita protested, though she was already untying her apron.

"You'll never be lazy," Gina said. "And see? I'm learning Spanish."

Juanita gave Gina a quick hug. *"Magnífico."*

"I say the men give the women a break and we do the cleaning up tonight," Bart said. "Then we'll serve the *tres leches* in the family room."

"Gosh darn, too bad I'll have to miss out on that," Zach teased as he reached over to muss the hair of one the twins. "The boys and I have business to take care of."

"Uncle Zach's teaching us rope tricks for the school talent show."

"And his timing is perfect, as usual," Matt said.

The other twin jumped from the table and started swinging his hand as if holding a rope. He knocked over a glass of milk in the process, and Becky jumped to clean up the spill before the liquid dripped onto the floor.

"That leaves three of us to take Juanita's place," Langston said, already walking to the kitchen with two empty platters in hand.

"Sounds about right," Matt said.

"Whew," Zach's twin sister Jaime said, faking a large sigh as the men disappeared with their hands full of dirty dishes. "We dodged that bullet."

"What's *tres leches?*" Jaclyn asked.

"Cake soaked in three kinds of cream. Jaunita uses evaporated milk, condensed milk and whipping cream," Becky said. "It sounds gross, but the texture of the cake is light with lots of air bubbles, so it doesn't get soggy the way you'd expect it to. If you've never had it, you're in for a treat."

"I'd never had it until Mom and Dad's wedding," Gina said. "Now it's my favorite dessert."

Jaclyn patted her full stomach. "Then I'll have to make room for a slice."

Gina excused herself to go out to the stables to see her favorite horse, leaving only Jaime, Becky, Trish and Jaclyn at the table. The small group of females seemed even more daunting to Jaclyn than the family en masse.

Jaime scooted to the chair next to Jaclyn. "You survived your first Collingsworth Friday-night dinner without running screaming into the night," Jaime said. "That's a big accomplishment."

"It wasn't so bad. Are Friday-night dinners different from other nights?"

"There are usually more of us at the table, and Juanita goes all out with the menu. It's a tradition that everyone show up at the table on Friday night—or they'd better have a very good excuse. Mom's big on tradition, and we humor her when it's not too painful."

"I look forward to our Friday-night family dinners," Becky said. "When I was with Nick, he went weeks during the playing season without having dinner with us."

"Nick's her husband," Jaime said. "He's a pro football player."

Jaclyn sipped her coffee as she studied the two sisters. The Collingsworth brothers were all exceedingly handsome, with dark hair, dark eyes and skin bronzed from the sun. Jaclyn imagined they must have gotten their looks from their father.

Becky and Jaime had definitely gotten their good looks, flawless skin and expressive blue eyes from Lenora. Jaime had strawberry-blond hair that fell straight until it reached her shoulders, then twisted into soft curls. She also had a great body and wore clothes that were a bit provocative, like the short black skirt that showed lots of leg and a soft white blouse that showed off her cleavage.

Becky was equally pretty but dressed and talked far more conservatively. She wore her short blond hair pushed back from her face—only bangs fell over the left side of her forehead.

Jaclyn's gaze shifted to Langston's wife, Trish. She was absolutely striking, with a heart-shaped face and dark hair that cascaded to her shoulders in loose curls. She had a glow about her, and when she looked at Langston, you could see the love in her eyes. Gina was a teenage version of her mother.

"Are you from a big family?" Jaime asked.

"No," Jaclyn answered, hoping they wouldn't get off on that track. "I was an only child."

"So was I," Trish said. "That makes close friends all the more special. I know how worried you must be about Margo. I hope you get a solid lead on her whereabouts when you visit Paradise Pastures tomorrow."

"Thanks."

Jaime's eyebrows arched. "Paradise Pastures? I thought your friend disappeared from New Orleans?"

"That's where she lived, but we have reason to believe she may have visited this area with a man she was seeing."

"Really? Who was she seeing?"

"Senator Pat Hebert from Louisiana."

Jamie made a face. "Sorry to tell you, Jaclyn, but he's married—and scum. He hits on anything with breasts. I hope your friend didn't get sucked in by his charm."

"Margo doesn't always make the best choices where men are concerned." It hurt to admit that, but there was more at stake here than Margo's reputation. "Do you know Senator Hebert?"

"Yeah. One of my friends hooked up with him one night at Cutter's Bar. He bought her a few drinks, they danced and then he got all bent out of shape when she wouldn't go back to the ranch with him. My boyfriend Garth and some of his friends sent him on his way. The man's bad news."

"I guess Margo didn't see that in him."

"Do you have a picture of her?" Jaime asked. "Maybe I've seen her somewhere around town."

"I have one in my purse." Jaclyn went to

get the snapshot they'd used on the flyers. She hated pulling Bart's family into this mess—but then, she'd done that just by being here. She hurried back with the photo and handed it to Jaime.

"This is your friend who's missing?" Incredulity colored Jaime's tone.

"Yes. Do you know her?"

"As a matter of fact, I do."

Chapter Eleven

Jaclyn's breath caught in her throat. It had never occurred to her that one of Bart's sisters would have met Margo. She scooted to the edge of her chair. "How do you know my friend?"

"Just from running into her a few times at Cutter's Bar."

"Are you sure it was Margo that you saw there?"

"Unless the girl in this snapshot has a twin. Only she goes by the name of Kelly."

Becky and Trish both leaned in closer. "If Jaime's seen her in town, then other people must have seen her, too," Trish said. "Someone may know where she is."

"She might still be around here," Becky said.

Jaclyn was afraid to get her hopes up, but she

was eager to know every detail. "Was Margo with Pat Hebert when you've run into her?"

"I've never seen her come in or leave with him," Jaime said, "but I've seen them dancing and drinking together. They get pretty intimate for a public place, if you know what I mean." Jaime returned the picture. "Did you know that she just had a miscarriage?"

Jaclyn sucked in her breath as a new shock wave rocked through her. "Did she tell you that?"

"She didn't tell me, but she told a friend of mine. My friend said Kelly came into the bar by herself on a weeknight with her eyes all red and swollen. After a few drinks, she started crying. When my friend asked her what was wrong, she spilled her guts about losing her baby."

"How long ago was this?"

"Two, maybe three, weeks ago. No, wait, it was October second. I'm sure of the date because I heard about it at another friend's bridal shower on the day after it happened. News travels fast in Colts Run Cross."

Three days after Jaclyn had gotten the e-mail saying how excited Margo was. She must have been talking about the pregnancy instead of a job. She'd probably thought that would push the senator into leaving his wife.

Jaclyn shuddered as new possibilities flooded her mind. She didn't know why Margo hadn't told her about the pregnancy, but a medical emergency like a miscarriage could explain why her house looked as if she'd just run out on the spur of the moment.

But that was three weeks ago. If she were all right, she would have surely gone home by now or at least contacted Jaclyn. Instead Margo had seemingly dropped off the planet.

The psychic's words seared their way back into Jaclyn's mind, and suddenly the thought of going to Paradise Pastures filled her with a suffocating, indefinable dread.

JACLYN, BART AND Langston arrived at the gate to Paradise Pastures at eight-thirty on Saturday morning. They'd discussed the possibility of Sheriff Guerra going along, but both Bart and Langston liked the idea of an informal meeting with Rene Clark.

"Looks as if the gate is unlocked," Langston said.

Jaclyn's anxiety level heightened. "Why would it be unlocked? Do you think this is a setup?"

"Nah," Bart said. "A lot of people around here don't bother with locks on their gates. We never did until we got the new remote-control system put in. Most people just latch them to keep them closed so they won't bang in the wind, as long as their horses are in a secured area."

"What about the cattle?" she asked. "Wouldn't they just walk out through an open gate?"

"You *are* a city girl," Langston said. "See that series of pipes with the gaps between them? It's called a cattle gap or cattle guard. The livestock can't cross them, so they stay inside even if the gate's left open."

"Makes sense. And, yes, I am very much a city girl."

Langston jumped out of the truck and opened the gate to let Bart drive through it. Once he was back in his seat, they started down a bumpy dirt road that led through scrubby underbrush and a string of pine trees.

Minutes later they pulled up in front of a

single-story brick house of pinkish stucco and wood. Like Bart's, it had a wide front porch with a swing, but no rockers or pots of blooming flowers.

"There are no cars or trucks around," Jaclyn said.

"Better for snooping," Bart said, already climbing out of the truck. "But this would be the main house where the owners stay when they're in town. The foreman's cabin is likely just down the road. Rene will probably show up soon enough."

Jaclyn followed the men up the walk, glancing behind her from time to time, half expecting the foreman and his posse of wranglers to show up with guns blazing. Neither Bart nor Langston seemed worried. Apparently she'd watched too many Westerns.

Bart tried the front door. "It's locked tight," he said. He knocked. When there was no answer, he put up a hand to ward off the sun's glare and peered through one of the front windows.

Jaclyn stepped next to him and did the same. The living area was furnished in dark rustic woods and maroon leather, all perfectly coordinated with pictures, throw pillows and table-size Western sculptures.

"Looks like a picture from one of those Western design magazines Mom's got around the house," Langston said.

"All the trappings of a weekend cowboy, right down to the black bear rug in front of the stone fireplace."

Jaclyn's stomach turned as she stared at the rug and imagined Margo entwined with Senator Hebert in front of a blazing fire, telling him she was pregnant. Had that been the trigger that led to her disappearance? The timing was perfect for it.

She moved away and walked to the side of the house to peer into another window. This one opened into a bedroom, also designer-perfect. Again the images that haunted her mind were much too disturbing. She backed away, then spun around at the sound of an approaching vehicle.

She hurried back to the porch as a white pickup truck skidded to a stop just behind Bart's truck. A tall, lanky man climbed out.

"That didn't take long," Bart said.

"Is that the foreman?" Jaclyn asked.

"That's him."

Jaclyn watched him approach. His face was whiskered, and his boots were coated in red clay. His jeans weren't much cleaner. She'd guess him to be near forty, but he could have been older. It was hard to tell with his face twisted into a disgusted scowl.

Rene stopped at the edge of the steps leading to the porch and spat a stream of brown gunk into the dirt. "You looking for someone?"

"You." Bart extended his hand, and surprisingly Rene took it. "I'm Bart Collingsworth from Jack's Bluff Ranch. We've met before."

"I remember."

"And this is my brother Langston and our friend Jaclyn McGregor."

Langston shook Rene's hand, as well. Jaclyn only nodded. She knew Bart was hoping to keep this friendly in the hopes of getting Rene to open up about Margo, but she had no desire to shake the man's hand, not when his body odor was noticeable from where she was standing.

"Actually, we were hoping to find Senator

Hebert here this weekend," Bart said. "Or his friend Margo Kite."

Rene rocked back on his heels. "Guess you're out of luck. The senator's not here, and I don't know anyone named Margo Kite."

Jaclyn pulled the picture from the side pocket of her handbag and held it up for him to see. "You may know her as Kelly."

He stepped closer. "Nope. Never laid eyes on her. Is this a personal call or business?"

Bart leaned against the porch banister and scanned the area for a few seconds before looking Rene in the eye. "I'm going to level with you, Rene. Margo Kite is missing, and the last place anyone saw her was at Cutter's Bar with Senator Hebert. I was hoping you or the senator would know where she is or where we could find her."

Rene hooked his thumbs in his front pockets and stared at the toes of his boots. "I don't know the woman, and there's no one here this weekend but me."

"What about your wranglers?" Bart asked.

"What about them?"

"I'd like to talk to them. One of them might know Margo."

"This is a small spread. I give the help weekends off. It's no sweat to handle things around here by myself."

"I don't guess you'd mind if we looked around a bit?" Langston said.

Rene's eyes narrowed. "You'll be wasting your time."

"Better we do it than have Sheriff Guerra get a warrant and bring a bunch of deputies out here to comb the house and ranch."

Rene spat again and wiped his mouth on the cuff of his shirt. "What makes you think the sheriff has grounds for a warrant?"

"Like I told you—several witnesses have claimed Margo was out here with Senator Hebert. It's common knowledge they were having an affair."

"Not to me," Rene said. "I don't keep up with who comes and goes with the ranch owners. That's their business. Mine's running the ranch."

"That's a good policy," Langston said. "But still, if the law finds a young woman disappeared after staying here for a few days, they might want to take you in for questioning, too."

Rene rubbed his right hand across his

whiskered chin, then shoved both hands into his pockets. "I'd tell the cops the same as I'm telling you—I don't know anything. But if you want to look around the property, knock yourself out. There's nothing here but a few cows."

"It would be nice to have a look inside the house as well," Bart said.

"The house is personal property. I can't let you in there without permission. But if you want to keep peering through the windows like voyeurs, go right ahead."

"Then I guess we'll just have to settle for that," Bart said.

"What did you say the missing woman's name was?" Rene asked.

"Margo Kite. Sometimes she goes by Kelly. If you've seen her or know anything about her, it would be better to speak up now. You don't want to get caught up in Senator Hebert's troubles."

"You're right about that. I don't get paid enough for trouble. But the thing is, I've never seen the woman. You can drive around the ranch all you want. Just be sure to latch the gate on your way out."

"He's lying," Bart said as Rene walked away. "There's no way he didn't notice a woman like Margo Kite."

"And probably every other woman they bring around." Langston peered through the window again. "I'll bet Margo's fingerprints are all over that house—not that prints will help unless hers are on file."

"They must be," Jaclyn said. "She worked at one of the casinos for a while, and they have all their employees screened to the max."

"Then all we need is for the sheriff to get his warrant and we'll know if she was here. We just won't know when."

"But it will prove that the senator is lying about knowing her," Jaclyn said. "Once that's out, he may as well talk. Unless…"

Unless he'd gotten rid of her for good.

"There's too much land here for us to even begin to cover," Langston said. "We may as well wait for the sheriff to get the search warrant and some good bloodhounds."

Jaclyn didn't argue the point, though the disappointment of finding out nothing new settled in her heart like a dead weight. She wasn't sure how many more dead ends she could bear.

"SHE SHOWED UP HERE today with Bart and Langston Collingsworth. I got rid of them pretty easily, but the Collingsworths worry me. I didn't count on them getting involved."

"They worry me, too. I never thought she'd find anyone who'd listen to her. This won't stop as long as Jaclyn is in the picture."

"I'm working on that. Having Bart Collingsworth sniffing at her heels every second isn't helping."

"I may be able to help you out with that."

"I don't need help. I told you I'd take care of it. Get the money ready. It's as good as done."

THE FOUR COLLINGSWORTH brothers gathered in the stables for an early-afternoon briefing on the latest developments in the saga of Margo Kite. Bart was the last to join them since he'd been on the phone with Sheriff Guerra for the last half hour and with Aidan Jefferies and Clay Markham before that. He brought a six-pack of cold beers with him.

Matt took one of the beers, dropped to the edge of a bale of hay and kicked his legs out in front of him. "How did the visit to Paradise Pastures Ranch go?"

"Rene denied ever having seen Margo at the ranch. All this lying add ups to a conspiracy in my book, a conspiracy that included luring Jaclyn to Colts Run Cross and then running her off the road to get her to keep quiet."

"We definitely may not have heard the last of that." Langston fed his last bite of apple to one of the horses. "So now it's a matter of keeping Jaclyn safe and waiting for Sheriff Guerra to come up with a search warrant."

"I just talked to him. He's working on it," Bart said. "The good news is that Aidan's found out that Margo's fingerprints are in the system from the casino job Jaclyn mentioned. So if the search warrant turns up her fingerprints anywhere in the house at Paradise Pastures, we'll have proof she's been there."

"None of which proves foul play," Matt said. "Margo could still have just walked away on her own."

"I'm glad you're not the judge in charge of issuing warrants," Bart said.

"I'm just playing devil's advocate."

"I'm playing the odds," Zach said. "I hate to say it, but I think there's a good chance Margo's buried somewhere on Hebert's ranch."

Bart took a long swig of his beer. "If it turns out like that, it will really hit Jaclyn hard. Her mother died when she was twelve and she never knew her father. Margo's like a sister to her, the closest thing she has to kin."

"She has you," Zach said. "Whether you've noticed it or not, you are falling for her like last month's stock market."

"I like her," Bart admitted. "I'm not pushing anything on her right now. She's already got too much on her plate."

"Wise thinking," Langston said. "Romance and a possible murder aren't the best of bedfellows."

Matt kicked at the loose hay beneath his feet and tugged his Stetson lower on his head. "Don't jump into anything with Jaclyn, Bart, not until you really know her. People can fool you. And she's not the kind of woman you're used to dating."

Bart took off his hat and dusted it against his leg—a habit when he was so mad he ached to aim his fist into someone's jaw. "Just say it straight, Matt. She's an ex-con."

"All I'm saying is be careful."

"Yeah, I will."

But right now he just wanted to be with her. So he'd do what any sane-thinking cowboy would do when he wanted quality time alone with a woman: he'd saddle up the horses and take her for a ride.

"YOU WANT ME TO GET on the back of that huge animal?"

Bart groaned. "Don't tell me you've never ridden a horse."

"Of course I have," Jaclyn said. "Only it was on a stick that made it go up and down and round and round to the music."

Bart made a show of covering the mare's ears. "Don't let Miss Tara hear you compare her to a carousel horse."

"I wouldn't. The carousel horse wasn't made for giants. Do you have something in, say, a size midget?"

"There's Killer back there. He's a hand shorter. And then there's Suicide. Now that's a ride."

"I'm thinking more like Cream Puff."

"Actually, Miss Tara here may be big, but she's the gentlest horse in the stables."

"Okay, cowboy. I just hope the air up there is thick enough that I don't get a nosebleed."

Bart smiled, amazed at how she managed a sense of humor in light of all she was dealing with. When he'd first asked her to go riding with him, she'd said no. It had taken all his persuasive powers to talk her into it.

"So where's the ladder?" she asked.

"No ladder." He placed the reins in her left hand. "Now just drape those over Miss Tara's mane and keep hold of them."

"Like this."

"Exactly like that."

He reached down and swiveled the left stirrup. "Now grab the back of the saddle with your right hand, and I'll give you a boost so that you can put your left foot in the stirrup. You do know what a stirrup is?"

"I've seen old Eastwood flicks."

"Thank goodness for Clint." He took her through the rest of the steps, and her mouth curled into a smile when she was finally settled in the saddle.

"Okay," she said. "Now lead me around the circle and then help me down. Or you can just help me down now and say I rode."

"No way. You're going to love this and beg for more."

"Wanna bet?"

He adjusted the saddle and showed her how to hold the reins and position her legs. "That's all there is to it. I'll keep my horse at a walk, and Miss Tara will stay right behind or beside me unless you kick her and give her full rein."

Jaclyn leaned low over the horse's neck. "Did you hear that, Miss Tara? We're going to walk very slowly. I won't kick you and you don't throw me. Deal?"

Miss Tara whinnied.

"I hope that meant yes."

Bart climbed into his saddle and the two of them rode—or rather, walked—out of the corral and down the path that led to the shallow creek that ran behind the stables. The day had started off overcast with rain clouds threatening from the west. But the sky was a bright blue now and the air was crisp, a perfect autumn day for a ride.

This is what a Saturday should be like—
a quiet ride under a sunlit sky with a beautiful woman at his side. Only there should
be no thoughts of missing women, adulter-
ous senators or murder hovering over them
like buzzards.

Not that he'd feel this awareness with just
any woman. Jaclyn got to him, and not just
sexually. He liked her smile, her way of
saying what she was thinking, her spunky
attitude. He liked the way her eyes lit up
when she laughed and the way she talked too
fast when she was excited or afraid. In fact,
he couldn't think of a single thing he didn't
like about her.

As for the ex-con bit, she said she was
innocent, and he believed her. But then, if
she'd said she'd just landed in a spaceship, he
might have believed that, too.

"This isn't nearly as bad as I feared,"
Jaclyn said, breaking the silence.

"Does that mean you want to go faster?"

"Maybe on the way back. Right now Miss
Tara and I are getting to know each other."

"If you lived on a ranch, you could ride any
time you wanted."

"Not a lot of ranches inside Shreveport city limits and within biking distance to the university. Speaking of transportation, I guess I should check on Margo's car."

"I had a call from Hank this morning."

"And Hank is?"

"Oh, that's right—you've had amnesia since we talked about Hank."

"Very funny."

"He's the mechanic who towed the car. The damage wasn't as extensive as I thought, so I told him to go ahead with the repairs. He's taking care of what's under the hood. A body shop in Conroe is taking care of the rest. I'm assuming Margo has some kind of collision insurance."

"That's a risky assumption, and I can't pay for those repairs, Bart."

"I'll take care of it. You can pay me later."

"No. I'm not a charity case. You had no right to do that without asking me."

She really was upset. He hadn't counted on that. "Look, I'm sorry. I thought I was helping."

"You are, but I can't just keep taking from you and your family when I have nothing to give back."

"You give back, Jaclyn." More than she knew. He stopped and dismounted near the creek. "Want to stretch your legs?"

"Is this just to change the subject?"

"Not entirely."

"Then, yes, I'd like to have my feet on the ground again."

He helped her from the saddle, and she walked toward the creek while he secured their mounts. By the time he reached the bank, she had one sneaker off and was untying the other.

"The water might be cold," he warned.

"Then I'll just wiggle my toes in it. It looks too tempting to resist."

He thought the same, only she was his temptation. Not the place or time, he reminded himself. Neither his mind nor body was listening.

Jaclyn rolled up her jeans and stepped into the water. "It's icy," she said, "but I like it." She started wading, stopping to roll her pant legs higher when the splash reached halfway to her knees.

He knew it was only temporary, but for now she seemed to have let her fears slip to the background. Bringing her here had been the smartest thing he'd done lately. He hadn't waded in the creek for years, but he dropped to a grassy area and pulled off his boots and socks. In seconds he was splashing through the water to reach her.

Her foot slipped in the mud as she turned to him. He caught her before she fell. She wrapped her arms around his neck, and the fragile hold he'd had on resistance disappeared like sand in the wind.

He pulled her closer and claimed her lips with his. He kissed her over and over, willing himself not to think of anything but her and how she felt in his arms.

His hands roamed her back, and he lifted her up only to let her slide down his body and over his arousal. He held his breath, fearing she'd pull away, but she held on to him while he lifted her again, this time letting his lips trail her neck to her cleavage.

His feet sank into the mud and he shifted to keep his balance.

Jaclyn pulled away. "That's enough, cowboy. I don't want to drown in a foot of water."

He tried to catch his breath as he led her to the bank. Every part of his body ached for her, but when he tried to tug her back into his arms, she pulled away.

"It would be a mistake," she whispered, and he knew she was talking about more than a kiss.

"Okay, but when this is over and life is back to normal, I want a chance at a relationship with you, Jaclyn."

She started to protest, but he stilled the words with a quick kiss. Even that he felt clear down to his toes. "Just a chance, Jaclyn. That's all I'm asking."

She nodded, but the light in her eyes had become shadowed, and he knew she was already pulling away, back into her nightmare world of Margo Kite.

But it wasn't Margo he was worried about. It was Jaclyn and the nagging fact that someone had almost killed her to get her to drop her investigation into her friend's disappearance. For all he knew, that person was still in Colts Run Cross and still had threats and murder on his mind.

The danger to Jaclyn would escalate as the

investigation heated up. A search warrant would fan the flames to a roaring fire. And the search warrant might be minutes away.

Chapter Twelve

It was midmorning on Monday before they got the news that Sheriff Ed Guerra had the signed search warrant in hand and had lined up a crime scene unit from Houston to check both the main house and the foreman's cabin at Paradise Pastures. The investigation now officially involved a Louisiana senator and the three prominent New Orleans business-men who owned the ranch with him. Guerra wanted no problems with claims of mishan-dling the investigation and he didn't have the manpower in his county to do the job as ef-ficiently as the big city CSU.

Bart had left the house shortly after the sheriff called, probably because he was too restless to stay inside with nothing to do. He'd taken one of the ranch's four-wheelers to the workshop to adjust the carburetor on the tractor they used to operate the baler. Jaclyn had no idea what that meant in terms of the actual task he was performing, but she was thankful to have him out of the house.

Being with him and not throwing herself into his arms had grown more difficult with every casual glance and incidental touch. The attraction between them was like a spark burning along a fuse and ready to ignite into fireworks at any second.

The passion filled her with guilt. How could she feel anything but fear and grief when she still didn't know whether Margo was safe or in danger? Even if she had been certain Margo was safe, giving in to her feelings for Bart could bring nothing but heartbreak. Her past would never let her fit into his world of wealth, family and social status. He could never fit anywhere else.

Still, she'd miss this place terribly when she went back to Shreveport. She'd miss Jaunita's cooking and Jaime's quick wit. Miss the twins' energy and Lenora's ever-present smile and positive spirit. Most of all she'd miss Bart.

Determined not to fall into the melancholy doldrums, she went to the kitchen to get a can of diet soda and the light jacket she'd borrowed from Jaime. If nothing else, a brisk walk would give her some exercise.

Her cell phone jangled as she opened the can. Her heart jumped as always with the hope it might be Margo. "Hello."

"Is this Jaclyn McGregor?"

The female voice was unfamiliar. "Yes?"

"I'm back from Europe and returning your call."

"Who is this?"

"Candy Hebert."

The senator's wife. She'd given up on ever hearing from her. "I'm glad you called."

"I don't want to talk on the phone. Can we meet somewhere?"

"I'm no longer in New Orleans."

"I know. The foreman at our Texas ranch said you'd been by to ask him about your friend who's missing. I'm at Paradise Pastures now, but I can't stay. The local sheriff has a search warrant—but then, you know that."

"Is that why you called?"

"Partly. Can you meet me in Colts Run Cross in, say, thirty minutes?"

"I'll have to call Bart. I'm not sure he can make it that quickly."

"I can't say what I need to in front of Bart Collingsworth, Jaclyn. You must know that this isn't easy for me. It's never easy on the wronged wife."

"Where do you want to meet?"

"There's a café on the corner of Main and Lancaster. I'll be at one of the outside tables."

"How will I know you?"

"I'm wearing black slacks and a yellow sweater and I'll have on sunglasses. It's important, Jaclyn. To both of us—and to my husband and Margo as well."

"Do you know where Margo is?"

"Yes. We'll talk at the café."

And that was it. Connection broken. The next move belonged to Jaclyn. Her first impulse was to call Bart, but if she did, he'd insist on going with her, which might totally defeat the purpose. Of course, there was a chance this was another setup like the one that had landed her upside down in a ditch.

Not likely but still too chancy. There had

to be another way, another place they could talk in private. And what was more private than Bart's house and Jack's Bluff?

Jaclyn pulled up the last number and punched the call button. Candy Hebert answered on the first ring. It took a little persuasion, but finally she agreed to Jaclyn's suggestion.

Jaclyn's stomach was twisting like a kite in a thunderstorm by the time she hung up the phone. She was afraid to get her hopes up, yet she couldn't hold them down. Hell hath no fury like a woman scorned.

And a woman scorned had every reason to tell all she knew about her husband's mistress no matter what the cost to the bastard who'd betrayed her.

CANDY HEBERT WAS attractive, sophisticated and impeccably dressed. She was the kind of woman Jaclyn would have thought men strayed to, not from. Her face was wrinkle-free, obviously BOTOXed or she'd had surgery. Her complexion was so smooth it looked as if it could have been poured on.

But as attractive as she was, she would have suffered badly in comparison with Margo.

Jaclyn had decided the kitchen, with its homey warmth, was the best place for their conversation. She poured two cups of tea and set one down in front of Candy. "Lemon or sugar?"

"Lemon," Candy said, reaching for a slice from the tray Jaclyn held out for her.

Jaclyn took the chair across from Candy. "You said you know where Margo is," Jaclyn said, unwilling to waste another second on stage setting.

Candy curled her fingers around her cup. "I know a lot about Margo Kite. Most of it isn't good."

"I'm not really interested in your opinion of her. I just want to find her and make sure she's all right."

"She's fine—and rich, thanks to the money made from her little blackmailing scheme."

"Margo has her faults, but she didn't blackmail your husband. She was in love with him and she thought he loved her."

Candy struck a pose, like an actress playing the part of angry, mistreated wife. "I can assure you that Margo Kite was in love with no one but herself. She set her sights on Pat from the first time she laid eyes on him. We were attending a private party in the home of a friend. Margo was supposed to be serving drinks. Instead she was shamelessly flirting with the male guests. She was fired before the night was over."

Jaclyn bit back the retorts that flew to her tongue. She didn't want to hear this. Yet she knew Margo was a flirt and had always enjoyed the attention of men.

"I'm sure she didn't force your husband to have an affair with her."

"No. I wish I could say Pat would never cheat on me, but he has, over and over again. The need to have sex with someone new and beautiful is almost like an addiction with him. Then he comes back to me ashamed and begging me to forgive him. I always do. You see, I love him too much to give him up."

Jaclyn refused to be reeled in by the act. "You need to talk to a professional counselor about this. My concern is finding Margo."

"I just want you to know what kind of woman your friend is. She stalked him day and night, called him, parked in front of our house, waited for him after work. He tried to break away from her, but she wouldn't let go."

"Where is Margo now?"

Candy twisted her napkin, then balled it in her hand. "Pat told her he'd admit his indiscretions with her and go to the police if she didn't get out of our lives. That's when she made up the story about being pregnant with his child."

"She wasn't lying about that. She lost the baby."

"She may have lost a baby, but it wasn't Pat's. He's sterile. That's why we don't have children."

Jaclyn felt like a traitor listening to these horrid stories about Margo. Yet the doubts were creeping in. Margo had been the only person Jaclyn had ever felt close to, the only one she'd trusted.

But she'd always had a side of her Jaclyn didn't understand. She could give so much so freely, but she needed a lot in return. She was the one who'd made constant phone calls to Jaclyn, wanting to be involved in every aspect of her life even when Jaclyn was struggling to keep on top of her job and her studies. Still, they were friends, and Margo had never let Jaclyn down.

Jaclyn's patience wore thin. "Just tell me where I can find her."

"She's gone—hopefully for good. I offered her money if she'd leave the country and never come back. She took it. She said she was going to St. Maarten. I'm not sure if she kept her word, but I haven't heard from her since."

"Why are you telling me this now?"

"Because I want you to call off the police."

"It's too late for that now."

"It's not too late as long as Pat's not in jail. Just say you were wrong. Say you heard from Margo and everything was a mistake. The police will back away and the media will have nothing to go with."

"How do I know you're telling the truth?"

"You know your friend. You must know better than any of us what she was capable of. Don't ruin my husband's career over a woman like Margo. I'm begging you, Jaclyn. If you have any decency at all, please don't steal my marriage and my life with your lies."

Jaclyn looked away and tried to gain some semblance of sense from all of this. How could Candy Hebert even want her husband back when she admitted he hit on women and had sex indiscriminately whenever he desired?

Candy might be telling the truth, but then again, it might all be the act it seemed. Margo could be in real danger. The psychic's words crept into Jaclyn's mind. She shivered and hugged her arms about her chest.

"I'm sorry, Candy. I'm not the one who ruined your marriage or the senator's reputation. This is all out of my hands."

Candy pushed the cup away as she jumped to her feet, sloshing the lukewarm tea onto Bart's antique table. "You're right, Jaclyn. It is now out of all our hands. Heaven help you."

Jaclyn stood on the porch and watched as Candy stamped down the short walk and scooted behind the wheel of her car. The words she'd said about Margo rang in Jaclyn's head. They might be all lies. They might be the truth.

Either way, Margo had been her friend, and Jaclyn would never forgive herself if she quit before she knew the truth of why she'd vanished without a trace.

But you're right, Candy Hebert. Heaven help me. And if you're lying and your husband killed Margo to keep her quiet, the way he did in the psychic's visions, heaven help us all.

JUST AS JACLYN HAD expected, Bart blew a fuse when he found out Candy Hebert had been in his kitchen with Jaclyn without his knowing about it. He'd lectured her sternly about the risks to her safety escalating now that this had blossomed into a full-scale investigation. Even now, hours later, with the two of them sitting on the screened-in back porch at the big house with Bart's mother and a neighbor named Billy Mack, he couldn't let it go.

Bart paced back and forth from one end of the wide porch to the other. "She had her nerve coming out here after she ignored Jaclyn's attempts to contact her when they were both in New Orleans."

"I'm sure she knew she'd be about as welcome as a tornado on a trail drive," Billy Mack said. "But it's over and done with now.

Besides, it would be nice if she was telling the truth and Jaclyn's friend is somewhere sipping one of them pink drinks with an umbrella on top. Did you hear anything from Sheriff Guerra on what the Houston CSU uncovered?"

Bart finally stopped his pacing and dropped to the wicker sofa next to Jaclyn. "I've talked to him a couple of times today. They found some women's negligees, condoms, sex toys, that sort of thing. It was a regular little cheaters' playpen. Fingerprinting may take a while. There were lots of different sets in the house, making it difficult to obtain clean, testable prints."

"It's all over the media now that Senator Hebert is a suspect in Margo's disappearance," Lenora said. "And there is a lot of speculation as to what his connection is to her."

"I hate that I've brought all this into your living room," Jaclyn said.

Lenora waved the comment off. "Nonsense. You didn't come looking for us. Bart went out and found you. I just hope this leads to some kind of resolution for you."

Zach stepped into the doorway from the

kitchen. "There is an unforgivable lack of activity in here," he said. "Are we fasting tonight?"

"I gave Juanita the night off," Lenora said. "It's her grandson's birthday and she's cooking for her family tonight."

"Are we invited?"

"You're invited to throw some steaks on the grill. I'll make a salad."

"Steak," Billy Mack said. "In that case, I accept your invitation to dinner."

Lenora tossed her hair, and Jaclyn could swear there was a hint of flirtatiousness in the movement.

"I don't remember inviting you to dinner, Billy Mack."

"No, but you would have gotten around to it. I saved you the trouble. I'll help Zach with the steaks. I've got a bit of news to share with him anyway."

"What kind of news?" Zach asked.

"We're getting a new neighbor."

"That's news to me, too," Lenora said. "Who is it?"

"Kali Cooper inherited her grandfather's spread, and I hear she's going to run it herself. Going into the horse business in a big way."

"I thought the old man disowned his family years ago," Bart said.

"Apparently he put Kali back in the will."

"I don't know why you'd think I'd be interested in anything to do with her," Zach said.

"She's about your age."

"And scrawny as a scarecrow. Hair like one, too, if I remember correctly."

Jaime joined them, dancing her way to the center of the room and then collapsing into a beanbag chair. "Who are you talking about?"

"Kali Cooper," Lenora said. "I remember her now. She had a crush on you, Zach. What was that, sixth grade?"

"Yes, and she was an annoying brat. If she asks, tell her I moved to China."

"Zach and Kali, sitting in a tree, k-i-s-s-i-n-g," Jaime serenaded, hand motions and all.

Zach picked up a couple of throw pillows and pelted her before disappearing back into the kitchen.

Billy Mack followed Zach. "I better see that he knows what he's doing. Don't want him messing up my steak."

"Billy Mack seems nice," Jaclyn said. "What's his story?"

"He's our closest neighbor," Lenora said. "His wife and I were best friends, saw each other practically every day back when we were raising our kids. I don't know how I would have made it after Randolph's death if she, Billy Mack and Jeremiah hadn't held me together."

"Where's his wife now?"

"Millie died three years ago. He's lost without her."

"He seems like a good man."

"One of the best. Millie and I were blessed. We married the men we loved, and the love never dimmed."

Jaclyn swallowed around an unexpected knot in her throat. "We should all be so lucky."

"Don't settle for less, Jaclyn. Don't ever settle for less. It isn't fair to anyone. Now I better go start that salad."

"I'll help."

"I'd like that."

Bart reached over and squeezed her hand, and the knot in her throat swelled to choking size. She had to tread carefully or she might start thinking she could actually fit into this marvelous family.

Bart groaned when his cell phone rang but took the call. She knew from his tone and the expression on his face that something was horribly wrong. She was trembling both inside and out when he broke the connection.

"A couple of teenagers were on their four-wheelers off one of the back roads near Paradise Pastures." He took her hand and squeezed it tightly. "They found a woman's body."

The words drained the life from her veins. "It's Margo, isn't it?"

"It's a female, auburn hair, early twenties. That's all they know."

"I want to see it."

"Better to wait until they get the body to the morgue."

"No, I want to see it just the way it was found. I want to know what that bastard did to her. And then I want to see him pay."

THE ROOM STARTED TO spin, and streaks of light shot out in every direction as if they were being flung by a giant monster with bloody hands. The psychic grew dizzy and her legs caved in on her, dropping her to the cold, hard floor of her shop.

Help me. Please help me.

She tried to help, but the invisible wall that separated her from the vision wouldn't let her pass through. All she could do was watch as the bullets dug gaping wounds into Margo's flesh.

She grabbed her head as white-hot pain tore her brain from the skull. And still she was being dragged along, through damp pine needles and slippery patches of mud.

Don't let me die. Please. Don't let me die.

But the darkness was closing in on her, gray at first but turning darker and darker until she was enveloped in the pitch-black shroud.

The pain stopped and the psychic peered beneath the blackness. Vacant eyes stared back at her. But this time the eyes were not Margo's. It was the eyes of Jaclyn McGregor who stared back at her from death.

The psychic came to slowly, weakened by the trance and still slightly disoriented. She stumbled to her desk and found the flyer. She had to call the nice woman who'd been so worried about her friend. She had to warn her before it was too late.

Chapter Thirteen

There were three squad cars parked along the back road, all with their lights flashing. Bart pulled up behind the back one. Jaclyn jumped out of the car without waiting for him to kill the engine. She ran along the edge of the road toward the cluster of cops who were standing beneath a towering pine tree.

"Hold it, lady! This is a crime scene."

Sheriff Guerra turned and waved. "It's okay. She may be able to identify the victim."

She saw the body then, laid out on what appeared to be a sheet of black plastic. The arms dangled to the sides at odd angles. One leg was twisted. The other looked normal.

She slowed, suddenly unable to feel her own arms and legs. Bart caught up to her and put an arm around her waist. "Steady, girl. I'm right beside you, and there's no rush."

She leaned on him, aware only that he felt strong and steady and safe.

Sheriff Guerra reached them a second later, flashlight in hand though it wasn't dark yet. "I hated to call," he said, "but no use to put it off."

"None I can think of," Bart said, "unless Jaclyn's not ready."

"I'm ready," she said.

Only she'd averted her eyes from the body when they'd gotten close and she hadn't convinced herself to look at it straight on yet. Not that she was afraid to find out it was Margo. She was certain that it was. Her fate had likely been sealed from the moment she became involved with Senator Hebert.

Bart kept his arm around her waist as they walked closer.

"There's some deterioration," the sheriff said, "but I don't think you'll have any trouble identifying the body."

Jaclyn lifted her gaze and took it all in at once. She nodded and turned away. "It's Margo. Margo Kite."

"You're sure?" Sheriff Guerra asked.

"Positive."

"The son of a bitch," Bart said, his tone leaving no doubt that he was referring to Patrick Hebert. "Go get him, Sheriff."

"Oh, I'll get him, all right. He screwed up royally when he brought his perversions and murdering ways to Texas. This time he's going down."

Jaclyn could hear the sounds all around her—cops calling out to each other, twigs cracking under their feet, the rustle of dry leaves being tossed by the light breeze and, somewhere in the distance, a dog barking.

And the muffled jangling of her phone from inside the pocket of her borrowed Windbreaker. Before tonight, she would have jumped to answer it. But now she knew it wouldn't be Margo calling to say everything was fine and she was sorry she'd been out of touch so long.

Jaclyn reached into her pocket and turned the phone off. "I'm ready when you are, Bart."

"You don't have to be so strong, Jaclyn. I'm here, and I'll take care of you."

"I'm okay. I just need to get out of here."

"You got it, baby. Let's go home."

BART WAS CONFUSED AND a little hurt by Jaclyn's reaction tonight. He wasn't sure what he'd expected, but more than the quiet resignation. It was as if Margo's death had taken the fight out of her and she'd pulled herself into her own little shell.

She hadn't needed him. That was what hurt the most. She didn't need him, but he needed her so much his arms ached to hold her. Not to make love. He knew it wasn't the right time for that. He just needed her to reach out to him. Instead she'd gone to her room almost immediately and hadn't come out again.

It was after midnight now. He was tired, but he knew he wouldn't sleep even if he went to bed. He'd just lie there and think of Jaclyn and wonder why he'd fallen so hard and fast for a woman who only gave him glimpses into who she really was. A woman who made a shield of her past and used it to keep anyone from getting close.

She claimed that Margo was the only friend she'd ever had, but he couldn't help but wonder how many people she'd kept on the other side of her invisible barriers.

His muscles tensed. He was getting nowhere. She didn't need him and that was that.

He walked out on the front porch and
dropped into the swing. They'd sat here on
that first day while she'd told him about
Margo. He'd sensed her vulnerabilities and
felt compelled to help her then.

But where were those vulnerabilities now?

I'm trouble, cowboy.

She'd called it right. And the trouble was
hitting him dead center in his heart.

JACLYN HAD FALLEN asleep almost the minute
her head hit the pillow, and that had been
within an hour after arriving back at Bart's.
He'd offered to cook for her or open a can of
soup if she wanted something light. She
hadn't wanted anything except to close her
mind to the stress and worry she'd lived with
for the last few weeks. Unfortunately the
sound sleep she'd fallen into hadn't lasted but
a few hours.

She looked at the clock again. Half past
two. She thought of Bart sleeping on the
couch while she tossed and turned in his

comfortable bed. She should trade places with him, but he'd never agree to it. He was a caretaker, warm and thoughtful, the kind of man she'd thought only existed in movies and fantasies.

It had been a miracle that he'd come into her life just when she'd needed a miracle most. She hadn't been able to save Margo, but she'd given it her best shot. So why couldn't she do the same for herself?

Instead she lay tossing and turning in a bed by herself when all she wanted to do was crawl into Bart's arms and give in to all the pent-up emotions that held her prisoner. Her fear of being hurt had been nurtured too long and it wouldn't let her take the risk of loving someone who wouldn't love her back.

But she would hurt anyway. She'd go back to Shreveport. He'd go on with his perfect life in his perfect family, surrounded by the kind of love she craved but would likely never have.

She kicked back the covers and slid her bare feet to the wooden floor. For once in her life, she wouldn't play it safe where her heart was concerned. She ached to feel Bart's arms around her—and she had nothing more to lose. She tiptoed to the door, opened it and padded into the living room.

"Are you having trouble sleeping?"

She jumped at the voice. Bart was sitting up in the dark, his feet propped on the coffee table.

"Yes," she said. "You, too, I guess."

"Haven't closed my eyes. Do you want some warm milk? Or I can make cocoa."

"I don't want anything to drink, but…"

"But what? Ask and it's yours."

She took a deep breath and released it slowly. "Make love with me, Bart."

"Why?"

"I don't want to be alone."

"Is that the only reason? Because if that's it, I'll hold you for as long as you like. You don't have to ply me with sexual favors."

"That's not the only reason." Her breath was shallow and her words refused to come out as more than a whisper. Asking for love was so new to her. "I need to feel you inside me, Bart. I need to feel passion and emotion and tenderness. I need to feel alive. Mostly I need you."

He crossed the room in an instant and swept her up in his arms. Neither of them uttered a word as he carried her to the bedroom, but his strength wrapped around her and she knew that nothing in her life had ever felt this right.

He placed her in the middle of the bed, then climbed in beside her, pulling her against him. They kissed for mere minutes— or an eternity—sweet, salty kisses that warmed her heart and made her hungry for more.

Their lovemaking was tender and gentle. Another time, it would have felt too tame, but tonight his soft touch and easy passion brought every part of her to life. He trailed his lips over her body, giving himself time to explore her thoroughly and giving her time to revel in the exquisite pangs of desire. His lips on her breast, his fingers finding her most erogenous areas, his body throbbing against her were a symphony of movements that brought her more sensual fulfillment in a few short minutes than she'd known in her whole life.

And then one quick thrust and he was inside her. Tears burned at the backs of her eyelids, and soft moans escaped her lips as he carried her with him over the top to a burst of passion and release that took her breath away.

"I came too soon," he whispered.

"No, Bart. You did everything exactly right."

"The right is us together, Jaclyn."

She snuggled against him, needing this night in his arms. But he was wrong about them. They would never belong together. Their pasts had shaped them—and their pasts were worlds apart.

Even if they could make things work, the family situation wouldn't. If she'd learned anything at all about the Collingsworths, it was that they held strongly to tradition and strict moral values. An ex-con would be an embarrassment. And eventually they'd turn against her. Bart might, too—and she could never bear that.

Tomorrow she'd do what she had to do, but she had tonight with her cowboy. And the memories would live forever in her mind.

"WAKE UP, PRINCESS Jaclyn. You can sleep through my kisses, but *nobody* gets to sleep through my bacon and eggs."

Jaclyn stretched and rubbed her eyes,

squinting from the bright sunshine that sprayed across the room. She tried to think about why she was in bed in the middle of the day, but her mind was floating in a fog. "What time is it?"

"Eleven forty-five."

"As in nearly noon?"

"You got it."

The events from the night before started to materialize in the haze left over from her deep sleep. Margo. And making love. The odd combination seemed bizarre in the morning light. "Why didn't you wake me?"

"I just did."

"I mean before now?"

"I tried. You didn't respond. I figured you needed the sleep. I know how hard last night was on you."

It was still difficult to believe Margo was actually dead, though at some level she thought she'd known it from her first day in New Orleans. Still, she liked waking to Bart. "Is that fresh-brewed coffee I smell?"

"Yes, along with bacon, scrambled eggs, wheat toast and Mom's homemade peach preserves." He set the tray on the side of the bed.

"Wow. I can't remember when I last had breakfast in bed. Wait—yes, I can. It was never." She sat up and reached for the coffee. The scent was almost as beneficial as the taste at pushing away the remaining dregs of sleep. "Aren't you eating?"

"I ate hours ago. I'm on rancher's hours. I have to go take care of some business in a few minutes, but I wanted to see you before I left. That's why I woke you."

"If it's about us and last night, don't…"

"It is about us, but first it's about news from the CSU investigation. They found Margo's prints in several places inside the main house."

Good news. She needed that. "What comes next?"

"Hebert's arrest. The warrant's already been issued and his attorney in Louisiana is bringing him in. It's all over the news this morning. He's playing down the affair with Margo but not denying it outright. He is denying having anything to do with the murder."

"The bastard." Still, she felt some measure of relief. He'd pay for the crime. It wouldn't bring Margo back, but at least there would be justice.

"I'm breathing a lot easier," Bart said, "knowing he's going to be behind bars in a matter of hours. Now we don't have to worry about his coming after you to keep you from spilling the beans on his affair with Margo."

She hadn't even thought of that. "I guess that means I'm free to go back to Shreveport."

"That's the other thing I wanted to talk about," Bart said. "I don't think you should go back."

That, she hadn't expected. "Why wouldn't I?"

"Shreveport's too far from Colts Run Cross. I know it's too early in the relationship for you to make any kind of commitment and I know Margo's murder has hit you hard, but I don't like the idea of you being that far away."

"I have another year at the university to earn my teaching degree."

"You can get your degree in Houston. There's Rice and U of H."

"You can't be serious about this, Bart. It's not like our relationship would have anywhere to go. I'm an ex-con. I'm not Collingsworth material."

"What the hell does that mean?"

Now she'd made him mad. She should never have made love with him. They shouldn't be having this discussion. "Can we talk about this later?"

"Sure. I have to get out of here now anyway. I won't be long and both Jaime and Zach are nearby. They said to call if you need anything at all, even if it's just company. Stay in bed all day if you want. I'll call you later. Or if you need anything, call me. I'm taking Zach's truck and leaving mine here for you in case you want to drive down to the big house."

He leaned over and kissed her goodbye. As if they were a couple. As if they could actually make this work.

As if she were Cinderella and had a rat's chance of having her dreams of love and family come true.

JACLYN'S STOMACH WAS in no mood to face food when Bart left, so she tossed breakfast down the disposal and grabbed a shower. She put on her third outfit and put the other two on to wash. Three sets of clothes to her name, all she could afford. If she didn't go back to Shreveport soon, she'd have to find a job here. Maybe Bart could put in a good word at Collingworth Oil for his ex-con girl-friend.

Her stomach tightened into knots. She had to stop this. It wasn't Bart she was mad it. It was herself for falling for him. She didn't want to leave. That was the problem. She wanted him to convince her to believe in miracles. Another night in his arms and he just might do it.

She heard a roar in front of the house. She hurried to the door. It was Jaime on the Harley Jaclyn had noticed parked at the big house. Jaclyn had assumed it belonged to one of the men.

Jaime pulled off her helmet and flipped her hair back into place with a shake of her head and a rake of her fingers. She waved to Jaclyn and took the steps to the porch two at a time. "Did you forget to pay your phone bill?"

"No, it's…it's turned off. I shut it off last night at the crime scene and forgot to turn it back on."

"Well, turn it on and give Bart a call before he has a heart attack worrying about you."

"Did he send you up here to tell me that?"

"Yeah, he said he's been trying to get you for half an hour."

"I'll give him a call right now. Do you want to come in a while?"

"If you feel like company."

"I won't be good company myself, but I could use some of your attitude."

"Have you been watching the news reports?" Jaime asked.

"I turned on cable news long enough to see Senator Hebert give an interview that made him sound like a saint who got mixed up with a devil woman. I turned it off after that."

"Then you didn't hear what they said about you?"

Jaclyn groaned. "Do I want to?"

"Probably not, but you'll like the performance by the senator's wife. She's fried a few brain cells—or as Billy Mack would say, if all her brains were ink, she couldn't dot an *i*."

"You can turn the set back on," Jaclyn said.

"I'll join you for the latest coverage after I talk to Bart."

Jaclyn dug the phone out from the pocket of her Windbreaker. There was one message waiting, so she called the voice mail number first. The message was from the psychic, and her words made Jaclyn's blood run cold.

"You are in danger, my dear. Grave danger. It's too late for Margo. You have to save yourself. Trust no one. Take no chances. And steel yourself against evil in its blackest form."

The psychic had called Margo's murder right, but there had to be a mistake this time. Senator Hebert was the blackest evil in Jaclyn's life, and he was going to jail. There was no one else to fear.

Still, the words haunted her when she phoned Bart. She assured him she was fine, but she didn't mention the call from the psychic. She wasn't sure why except that talking about it would make it seem more real.

She joined Jaime in the den and dropped to one of the chairs in front of the TV just as Candy Hebert's face popped up on the screen.

The interviewer asked her if she believed her husband had killed Margo Kite, and the first words out of Candy Hebert's mouth were, "Jaclyn McGregor."

"She hates you," Jaime said as the woman went on and on about how Jaclyn had started the rumors that her husband was having an affair with Margo.

"Turn it up," Jaclyn said.

"Maybe we should turn it off."

"No, I want to know what the whole country is hearing about me."

"Jaclyn McGregor was released from prison just one month ago. You can check the records. She's a convicted thief, and the money she stole was never returned. She's the one who should be arrested. She's the one with motive to kill Margo Kite."

"What is that motive?" the interviewer asked in a tone that suggested she was buying into Candy's theory.

"She tried to blackmail Patrick, and when he wouldn't pay her off, she made up the vile stories about him. Her boyfriend, Bart Collingsworth, was in on it with her. He has influence with the local sheriff in that little cowboy town and he had the victim's prints planted in our ranch house to slant the blame toward Patrick."

"Oh, no," Jaime wailed. "She would have to bring Bart into it. He's going to blow a fuse when he hears this. And God only knows what Mother is going to do. And Langston hates any kind of bad publicity attached to the oil business."

Nausea hit in waves, practically sending Jaclyn to her knees before the fury checked in and helped her fight it off. The Collingsworths had shown her nothing but kindness and now they were getting kicked in the gut for having done it. And Bart, her sexy, sweet cowboy with the mesmerizing smile, was getting the brunt of it all.

She didn't know how the Collingsworths would react to this, but she knew she had to get out of their lives before Jack's Bluff was crawling with media.

"I need a favor, Jaime."

"Sure."

"Give me a ride to the nearest bus station so I can get the hell out of Dodge before I cause your family any more trouble."

"Bart will kill me if I do that."

"He won't kill you. He'll be glad. My leaving will make things better for him and for your whole family."

"I don't think so," Jaime argued. "My family won't like the media attention, but they never back down from a fight."

"It's not their fight, Jaime. It was never their fight. You have to give me a ride to the bus station, and I'll be out of here. I was leaving anyway. I'll just be leaving a day or two sooner than expected."

"Bart's crazy about you, Jaclyn. You like him, too. I see it in your eyes when you're near him. It will hurt him a lot if you just run out on him without talking to him about it first."

"You're right, Jaime. I like your brother a lot. I might even be in love with him. And that's why I have to go. If we're meant to be together, it will work out in the end."

Jaime walked over and put her arms around Jaclyn. Jaclyn held on tight—but only for a minute. If she didn't get out of here quick, Bart would hear the news and come rushing back. Then it would be too late.

"Okay," Jaime said. "But we'll have to stop by the house for the other helmet."

"Then let's leave now."

RENE CLARK WAS PARKED in the tree line along the side of the road, out of sight but where he could watch whoever entered or left Jack's Bluff Ranch. He heard the Harley before he saw it. He'd expected it to be Bart's sexy younger sister. He hadn't expected her to have a passenger riding behind her.

But there she was, just as Candy had predicted. Running away to keep from dragging her boyfriend into danger.

That was awful sweet of her. Too bad she wouldn't live long enough to get any kudos for her thoughtfulness.

Chapter Fourteen

Bart left the Cattlemen's Association Board meeting as soon as he finished presenting the proposition he'd spent the last few months writing and refining. If he hadn't shown up today, it would have been another year before he could have introduced the much-needed changes. He knew Jaclyn was in good hands back at Jack's Bluff and probably even needed the time alone. Still, it had been incredibly difficult to leave her alone this morning.

He'd never believed in love at first sight, but he had fallen for Jaclyn in record time. It was almost as if his heart had been lying dormant until she came into his life. He had no doubt that she was the woman he wanted to spend the rest of his life with. He only hoped he could keep his feelings under control so that he didn't frighten her off before she realized that she loved him, too.

She had to love him. Nothing could feel this right and be wrong.

His phone rang before he made it to Zach's truck. It was Langston.

"I'm glad I caught you," Langston said.

Langston's tone set off a few warning bells. "I just got out of a meeting. Is there something new with Pat Hebert's case?"

"Oh, there's something new all right. Your name is being bandied about every major news channel. They're calling you everything from an accessory to murder to an underhanded billionaire."

"What did I do to deserve such praise?"

"It's not funny, Bart. I just caught some of the news coverage. Pat Hebert's wife is being interviewed by any and everyone who can stick a camera in front of her face."

"What's her claim to fame?"

"She's explaining how you helped conspire with Jaclyn to blackmail Pat Hebert and used your influence with Sheriff Guerra to plant Margo's fingerprints in the house at Paradise Pastures."

"And exactly why did I do those vile and underhanded things?"

"To steer the blame away from your girl-friend."

"Which would be Jaclyn?"

"So claims Mrs. Hebert, and she's getting a lot of mileage out of the accusations."

Bart muttered a curse. This was the last thing he needed, the last thing any of them needed, especially Jaclyn. He ended the conversation with Langston as quickly as he could and tried to reach her. No answer—and she'd promised to keep her phone on and handy after the morning's debacle. He left a message, then jogged the last few yards to his truck.

His phone rang again as he was gunning the engine to life. He answered the call.

"Howdy, Bart."

"Afternoon, Sheriff. If you're calling to tell me I'm replacing Paris Hilton as the hottest story around, I've already heard."

"That's old news. I figured you'd heard that hours ago."

"Nope. Just got out of a meeting. What's the update?"

"Bad news. The case against Patrick Hebert is stretching thinner by the minute."

"How so?"

"The coroner is estimating Margo's death somewhere between nineteen and twenty-three days ago. Pat Hebert was out of the country during that period, trying to line up foreign commercial investors for post-Katrina New Orleans."

"Maybe the coroner is off by a few days."

"That still would leave the issue of the lie-detector test that Hebert took an hour ago."

"What did he lie—or not lie—about?"

"He indicated that he didn't kill Margo, that he was in love with her and that when she became pregnant with his baby he told his wife that he was going to divorce her and marry Margo. The verdict is that he was telling the truth on all counts."

Bart took a right turn onto the I-45 frontage road. "That's interesting, since Candy Hebert told Jaclyn that her husband was sterile and that was the reason they didn't have children."

"I'd like to get Candy Hebert hooked up to a lie-detector test. Which reminds me of one more fascinating little detail to the case. Apparently she and the senator had separate checking and savings accounts. Hers were by far the fattest since she'd gotten her funds the old-fashioned way."

"From Daddy dearest?"

"And Grandpa. He was a restaurant mogul. Daddy followed suit. Anyway, Candy Hebert had several million dollars transferred to a bank in the Cayman Islands."

"When was that?"

"Last week."

"Sounds as if she may be planning a trip abroad, maybe a very long trip."

"Like the rest of her life," the sheriff agreed. "I'm having all the commercial airlines leaving the area for foreign destinations monitored, but it's impossible to monitor private planes flying into Mexico."

"So says Homeland Security."

"Right. I've gotta run," Guerra said. "I just wanted to touch base and keep you posted."

"I appreciate that. Later." He broke the connection with Ed and tried Jaclyn's number again. Still no answer. A niggling apprehension crawled under his skin.

"C'mon, Jaclyn. Answer the damn phone. Please."

JAIME PARKED HER motorbike in front of a mom-and-pop sandwich shop in Colts Run Cross. She pulled off her helmet and waited for Jaclyn to do the same.

"It's not much of a bus stop," she said. "Just that little sheltered bench around the corner there. But it's the nearest one. You buy your ticket from the driver. I think they post a schedule on the wall behind the bench. I'll go with you to check it out since there's no use in your hanging around if it's going to be hours until the next bus comes."

"I appreciate this, Jaime."

They walked to the bus stop together. Jaime checked the schedule for buses going north. "There's nothing to Shreveport until tonight, but there's one to Dallas due through here in the next ten to fifteen minutes—if it hasn't already come and gone. You can take that north and then get another bus east to Shreveport."

"Sounds like a workable plan."

"I'm going in the sandwich shop for a soda. Do you want me to bring you one?"

"No, thanks. I'm fine."

"Okay, but I'm starting to think this is a really bad idea. Why don't you change your mind, Jaclyn, and go back to Jack's Bluff with me? There's safety in numbers—and you know we've got the numbers."

"I'll be fine. The danger is past."

"Then just stay until you talk to Bart."

"We've already talked about this, Jaime. You know that my leaving is for the best."

Jaime shrugged. "I guess. I'll get my drink and hang out with you until the bus comes, just in case you change your mind and decide to go back to the ranch with me."

"I won't."

There was a line in the shop, and with only one person making sandwiches and taking orders, it was a slow process. Finally, Jaime got her soda, but by the time she made it back to the bus stop, there was no sign of Jaclyn. Obviously, she'd caught the bus. Poor Bart. He'd be bummed, but he could go after her and bring her back. True love prevails and all that jazz.

In the meantime, Jaime had to get home and change into something sexy—just in case she got interviewed by the media. If she was going to be seen by millions of people, she definitely wanted to look hot.

She started back to her motorbike just as the bus to Dallas rounded the corner. It slowed, then stopped a few feet behind the bench. Two elderly men got off. No one got on.

So where was Jaclyn? There was no way this could be good.

JACLYN TRIED TO FOCUS, but her eyes felt as if they were coated with grease. She had a splitting headache to go with the vision problems. The rest of her was numb.

Her head bounced and came down hard on what she thought must be the backseat of a car. But whose car? And why was she on the floor?

She opened her mouth and tried to talk, but her tongue was so heavy she could barely move it.

Margo. Bart. A bus stop. Words and images darted around in her confused mind like drunk wasps.

"You still alive back there?"

Rene Clark. And a needle. A few thought fragments congealed into a whole. She'd been waiting on a bus. Rene Clark had stopped and…and plunged a needle into her arm.

"Youuu…drru…" The words wouldn't come out.

"Don't worry—the effects will wear off soon and then the real fun will begin."

She stopped trying to talk. She'd need all her strength to escape. The car picked up speed and the bouncing became more intense. Her mouth hit against the back of the driver's seat so hard that she tasted blood.

She tried to brace herself, but she couldn't move her hands or her legs. They must be bound, though she had no sensation of pain at her wrists or ankles.

She missed Bart, missed his voice, his touch, his strength, his smile. She'd never even dreamed there were men like him in the world. He'd taken her under his wing, and unless she was extremely mistaken, he'd taken her into his heart. But none of that changed the danger she was in now. He'd think she'd caught a bus to Dallas, believe she was running away from him and any chance to make their relationship a lasting one.

She'd have to find a way out of this on her own.

"I ASKED EVERYONE around here if they saw Jaclyn get into a car with someone. No one has."

Bart's frustration with Jaime and the situation rivaled his anxiety, both of them flying off the charts. "I just wish you'd called and told me what she was planning before she disappeared."

"It's not my fault, Bart. She begged me to bring her here. She's old enough to make her own decisions. It's not like she's a runaway kid."

"I know. This is probably more my fault than anyone's. I should never have gone to that stupid meeting."

"Do you want me to keep hanging around the bus stop in case someone brings her back here?"

"No. Go on back to the house. Stay with Mom and Becky and help them deal with the media frenzy. Don't let Jeremiah take a rifle after the reporters."

"I think Candy Hebert is behind this, Bart. She hates Jaclyn. Anybody can tell that just by listening to her on TV."

Right, and she'd hated Margo Kite, too.

And possibly Tiffany Sparks, as well. That was the reason there was no time to waste. And wasting time was all he was doing until he figured out where to look.

Where would Candy Hebert take someone where she wouldn't be seen? Somewhere she'd feel safe? Not anywhere on Paradise Pastures. There were too many cops and media personnel hanging out there. So what did that leave?

Only about a hundred isolated roads and thousands of acres of wooded area just like the place they'd found Margo's body. He couldn't cover them all, but…

But he had to find her. He couldn't lose her, not like this. Not to a killer who's gone totally mad.

THEY'D TURNED ONTO A back road, and the canopy of branches grew so thick that Jaclyn could barely see the sun. She could think a bit clearer now, though she could still feel the lingering effects of the drugs, and her muscles and joints ached from the constant jostling and body slamming.

The car slowed and came to a stop. "Where are we?" she asked.

"The end of the line." He laughed at his callous joke. His cackle reminded her of one of the prisoners on her floor who'd gone mad and finally found a way to kill herself, laughing all the while.

"Have you ever been in prison, Rene?"

"No, but I hear you were. Why don't you tell me about it?"

"If you kill me, you'll find out soon enough for yourself."

"Wrong. Prison is for losers. Me, I'll be on a beach in the Caribbean, lying in a hammock while some brown-skinned island goddess takes care of my every need."

"Then why aren't you there now? You killed Margo. Where's your payoff for that?"

"It's coming, Jaclyn McGregor. Don't you worry your pretty little head about that."

He opened his door and stepped out. This was it. He was going to kill her the same way he'd killed Margo. Eventually some kids or hunters would stumble over her body and call the authorities. Someone would tell Bart.

Her heart twisted, and she bit her bottom lip to keep from crying.

Don't go back to Shreveport.

It's all Bart had asked of her. She'd blown it off as a ludicrous, impossible request. He'd asked for a chance at a relationship. She'd thought it too risky. Not because she might not grow to love him but because she already did and didn't want to face the pain of having loved and lost.

Rene opened the back door just as another car pulled up and stopped beside them. There was no surprise at all when Candy Hebert stepped out of the second car and walked over to join them.

"Ah, Jaclyn, how nice to see you again. We had such a pleasant conversation the last time we were together. Do you remember how it went? Me, groveling. You playing the Collingsworth card as if it had been dealt to you instead of stolen off the bottom of the deck."

"I didn't play card games with you, Candy. I wanted to know what happened to Margo. But I can see why you wouldn't want to say

that you and Rene had killed her. I suppose
Win Bronson was in on this with you."

"Indeed not. He's far too naive to believe
me capable of murder. He thinks I paid
Margo to leave town and he's merely trying
to keep his boss's lurid little affair a secret.
Take her out of the car and untie her, Rene."

"I don't see the use of untying her, but I'll
definitely take her out of the car. I don't want
her blood found in it. It was bad enough when
I had to unload the car I used to run her off the
road."

So that was Rene, too. All the things she'd
blamed on the senator had stemmed from the
murderous jealousy of his wife and her
assassin handyman.

"Take her out and untie her. I give the
orders. You take them."

His hands tightened into fists, and Jaclyn
realized it was all he could do not to slam
them into Candy's face. If she could get him
even more upset—so furious that he'd turn
against Candy—Jaclyn might have at least an
outside chance at escape.

"So you do all the dirty work," Jaclyn said
as he yanked her out of the car and propped

her against the back fender. "The one who pulls the trigger is the one who goes to prison."

"Only if they get caught. I don't intend to stick around that long."

"Is the plane ready?" Candy asked.

"It will be by the time we get back there. As long as I have my money."

"When the job is done."

Which meant when she was dead. Jaclyn had to keep them talking. "Why Margo, Candy? Why Tiffany Sparks? Why them and not all the others your husband slept with?"

"Tiffany because she was the first and I thought my killing her would frighten him into fidelity. What a joke that was." She pulled a penknife from her pocket, stooped and cut the tape that bound Jaclyn's ankles. "Margo because she was giving him the one thing I couldn't."

"His baby," Jaclyn said as the most pathetic side of Candy's illness finally registered in her mind. "You were the one who was sterile, weren't you? And the senator was going to give up his career and you for Margo and the baby. It was just as Margo said."

"He was my husband, Jaclyn. Mine. I was

not going to give him up to some two-bit whore with a womb."

"But you'll let him go to prison for your crimes."

"He'll go to prison for driving me to what I did." Candy stepped behind Jaclyn and slid the cold blade of the knife against her wrists, then sliced through the tape, freeing her hands.

Only one thing held her captive now and that was the gun that Rene had just pulled from his shoulder holster and aimed at her head. The words of the psychic screamed in her mind, and she realized now that the black evil of death was Candy Hebert. Too bad the psychic couldn't have called her by her name.

"Get on your knees, Jaclyn," Candy said.

"Wait." Rene shoved Jaclyn against the car and stood in front of her as the whir and thump of a helicopter flew over the treetops.

Rene pressed himself against her, hiding her with his body until the copter flew past. It seemed to linger in the area before the sound finally faded to silence.

"I said to drop to your knees," Candy said,

yelling as if the copter were still drowning out her voice.

"Are you crazy?" Rene yelled. "That helicopter pilot had to see us. I'm shooting Jaclyn right here in the street and we're getting out of here now."

"I always make them pray first. You know that I can't kill them until they pray for forgiveness for their sins."

"To hell with her sins. To hell with both of you."

Now or never, Jaclyn decided. This was the best chance she was going to get. Rene's concentration was so focused on Candy that the aim of the gun had shifted.

Jaclyn moved swiftly, bringing her knee into Rene's crotch and going for his eyes with a hard thrust of her outstretched fingers. She couldn't wait to see if the attack had been successful. She was on the move the nanosecond after she'd struck, running hard for the tree line and diving headfirst into the brush.

A bullet sent clods of earth flying about her head, but she was up and running again, zigzagging from one tree to another until her lungs burned and her legs felt like lead.

The heavy, stamping footsteps stayed close behind her. Another shot rang out, and this time the bullet hit so close to her head that the shattering bark cut into her like dozens of little knives.

She started to run again, but her foot caught on a tree root, and she went down face-first, her hands sliding across the ground. When she looked up, Rene was standing over her, the pistol pointed at her head.

Somewhere in her mind she heard the heavy clanging slam of a metal door. But this time it would have slammed shut on all her hopes and dreams. Her biggest regret was that she'd never told Bart that she loved him. She closed her eyes and waited for the end.

The gun cocked. "Say goodbye, Jaclyn."

Chapter Fifteen

"I really wouldn't do that if I were you."

Jaclyn's eyes flew open, though she wasn't sure if she was dead or dreaming.

Rene planted a foot on her chest, pinning her to the ground. The gun remained pointed at her head, but his gaze had moved to a spot off to Jaclyn's left. It was Bart, with a pistol pointed at Rene.

"I'd say we have a Mexican standoff," Rene said.

"You might want to think again."

This time the voice came from her right. She stretched her neck until she saw Langston with his pistol pointed at Rene's head.

"I'd say that, one way or another, you're going down, Rene Clark."

"So I may as well take the lady out with me."

"If you're tired of living." The third voice came from behind Jaclyn. She couldn't see the speaker, but she recognized Matt's voice. The last Collingsworth brother she would have expected to come to her rescue.

Something rattled the branches just over Rene's head. He jumped back and threw his hands up to ward off a small twisted limb that looked a lot like a rattler. The limb and Rene hit the ground in a thrashing crash of wood and man.

Jaclyn wasn't sure what had happened until she saw Zach on top of Rene, wrestling the gun from his hand. He'd ambushed Rene while he'd been fighting off a harmless limb.

She struggled to her feet. By the time she made it, she was in Bart's arms, holding on tight, while the million questions she had about the daring rescue were lost in the thrill of his kiss.

SHERIFF GUERRA'S SQUAD car was parked behind Rene's and Candy's cars when they exited the wooded area. Rene was being herded by Zach and Langston and their pistols.

"We've got Rene, but I'm afraid we lost Candy Hebert," Bart said.

"Naw, she's in the back of the squad car in her new silver bracelets. She was running from the trees and up to greet me when I drove up."

"She was the one who had Tiffany Sparks killed, too," Jaclyn said. "She admitted everything. I only wish I'd gotten it on tape."

"I don't think we'll need it. This attempt on your life pretty much seals the deal, and the medical examiner has reported lots of skin underneath Margo's fingernails. I suspect we'll have both Rene's and Candy's DNA to prove their presence at the crime scene. And the senator's champing at the bit to plea-bargain at the expense of his loving wife."

Guerra's deputy walked over and fastened a pair of cuffs on Rene, relieving the Collingsworths of their law-enforcement duties.

"Guess you guys are going back in the copter," Guerra said.

"Might as well. That's where our cars are."

"I'll send someone to pick up these two cars." The sheriff walked over to Jaclyn and raked a clod of dirt from her arm with the edge of his thumb. "Are you sure you're all right? No amnesia this time?"

"No amnesia."

"Well, I'll say one thing for you—you sure got some cheerleaders in the Collingsworth family. And not just these blokes, either. Lenora, Becky, Jaime—they were all panicking when you disappeared. Even old Billy Mack called to give me some instructions on how to find you. Not that I paid him no never mind."

"It's nice to have cheerleaders," Jaclyn said. That was pretty much the understatement of her life. She scanned the area. "Where is this helicopter you keep talking about? I saw you fly over, but I thought you'd left after that."

"We're just down that incline and past those tall pines," Langston said. "And I say we get started in that direction. I got a wife waiting on me at home."

"Oh, rub it in," Matt lamented. "I've got a couple of turtles, some lizards and an armadillo living behind my house, and you don't hear me bragging."

Zach clapped Matt on the back. "You the man."

"It's a lot longer walking back than it was running over here," Langston said. "It's amazing what a bucketload of adrenaline can do."

"I still don't get all of it," Jaclyn said. "Where did you get the helicopter? Don't tell me the Collingsworths own it?"

"Not this one," Langston said. "Ed Guerra commandeered it from the state police because it was already in the area. But Collingsworth Oil owns a small jet and a helicopter. They're used a lot. It saves the company money in the long run."

"And the small, snaky limb that fell on Rene's head," Jaclyn said. "How did you pull that off? I know it wasn't fate."

"Fate may have had a small part in it," Zach said. "My hurling arm's not what it was in my college baseball days."

"So you just tossed it into the tree and it came down on target?"

"What can I say? We did win the College World Series my junior and senior years."

The Collingsworths really were amazing. They finally reached the helicopter. It looked a lot bigger on the ground than it had in the air. Jaclyn looked around for a pilot but didn't see anyone.

Bart crawled in first and extended her a hand. She hesitated. "Who's going to fly this thing? And don't tell me one of you won a model-plane-flying contest in tenth grade and learned how to use the controls."

"I didn't actually win," Langston said, "but I came in third."

She gave up. Who knew when to believe them? Langston took the controls and it was evident he knew what he was doing. Bart tugged her to the back of the craft and pulled her into his arms. He kissed her and held her close.

"I've never been half as scared as I was when I saw that gun pointed at your head. Do you know how close I came to losing you?"

"How close we came to losing each other," she whispered.

"Are you really okay, Jaclyn?"

"I'm a little sore but glad to be alive."

"I hate it that this hit you so fast. You were still in grief and then this came at you."

"Grief doesn't have a shelf life. I have plenty of it left. It will come and go, but I hope that one day I can remember the good without the horror."

"I shouldn't have come at you like I did this morning. I knew I should give you time. I just couldn't stand the thought of you living so far away." He kissed her again. "I still don't want you to go."

"I could stay, but I'd need one big concession."

"I could get you your own place if you want. You don't have to live on Jack's Bluff."

"That's not the concession. I love you, Bart Collingsworth. I've never said that to anyone in my life. I know we're new together and have a lot to learn, but I know that there's nothing that could make me stop loving you."

"I feel the same. I love you so much, Jaclyn McGregor. Love you more than life itself—I found that out today."

"Then marry me, Bart. Marry me, any day you say."

"Oh, God, Jaclyn. You're not teasing or putting me on? You wouldn't do that to me, would you?"

"Never."

He leaped into the air and sent his Stetson

sailing across the copter. "Did you hear that, guys? I am getting married!"

A cheer went up that rocked the craft. Fortunately Langston stayed at the controls.

Bart pulled her back into his arms. "Marry me, marry my family."

"You've got yourself a deal, cowboy. Just as long as there's a lock on the bedroom door."

"We heard that!"

Bart just smiled as she settled back in his arms. A man she loved with all her heart and a wonderful family that saw beyond her past and opened their arms to her. Finally, she belonged. Proof beyond a doubt that dreams really could come true.

* * * * *

*Turn the page for a first look
at the next book in the*
**FOUR BROTHERS
AT COLTS RUN CROSS** *series*
*POINT BLANK PROTECTOR
Coming February 2008
Only from Harlequin Intrigue*

Prologue

The night was pitch-black when Kali Cooper stepped out of her mud-encrusted Jeep to open the gate to the Silver Spurs Ranch. *Her* ranch.

She still hadn't quite gotten her mind around the fact that she was the actual owner of the spread she'd grown up loving. But, after months of court battles with the son of her late grandfather's third wife, it was official. Grandfather Gordy's will had been clear and absolutely legal. As long as she lived on the land for a year, it was hers. She planned to live here forever.

The wind cut through her denim jacket and she could smell the approaching rain. She picked up her pace as lightning cut a jagged scar across the night sky followed by a loud clap of thunder.

The weather channel had predicted a line of moderate to severe storms followed by an arctic cold front that was dipping all the way to the Gulf of Mexico and bringing with it temperatures near the freezing mark. Even for mid-February, that was cold for the Houston area.

Wings fluttered above her and something rustled the grass to her left as the gate swung open and clanked against the metal post. An eerie uneasiness crept along her nerve endings along with the awareness of just how alone she really was. The closest ranch was Jack's Bluff and even as the crow flies, that was over a mile away.

She hurried back to the Jeep, drove across the cattle gap then jumped out to close and latch the heavy metal gate. This time she steeled herself not to be spooked by the sounds or creatures of a dark Texas night.

Five minutes later, she pulled up in front of the old homestead. Caught in the ghostly glow of her headlights, the one-story structure seemed to crawl out at odd angles and gables from the front porch. It was smaller than she remembered it, but thanks to the feud between her father and grandfather, she hadn't been here since she was eleven.

That was the summer she'd experienced her first case of serious puppy love. The object of her affections had been Zach Collingsworth, and she'd fawned and drooled over him like the naive kid she'd been. Hopefully he wouldn't remember her. With luck, he'd also be paunchy and balding, with a wife and several kids.

She reached for her flashlight and was about to kill the engine and cut off the lights when she saw what appeared to be a person running from the house. She hesitated, but when another streak of lightning made the scene as bright as day, all she saw were tree branches swaying in the wind.

She really was letting the isolation get to her. The house was empty and had been for months. The livestock had been sold and the help let go when her grandfather had died.

She stepped from the car just as lightning struck again, this time a dazzling needle of electricity that followed a direct path from sky to ground and seemed to strike mere yards away. The thunder that followed was deafening.

The first drops of rain pricked Kali's face as she made a wild dash for the covered porch. She was stamping the mud from her boots when her gaze caught and held. She stared, at first not willing to believe her eyes, but the trail of crimson drops leading to the door was all too real.

Her heart slammed against her chest, and this time she didn't try to convince herself she was imagining things. She started to run and was almost to her car before her powers of reason pushed through the adrenaline rush.

Paint—not blood. That was it, of course. She sucked in a huge gulp of damp air as the picture became crystal clear. Hayden Carpenter only lost the ranch to her if she lived here for a year. He probably planned to make sure she didn't last a night so he'd come out here with his Halloweenish tricks to frighten her away. Nice try, but it wouldn't work.

Bracing herself for what she'd find inside, she marched back to the porch and turned the doorknob. As she expected, the door was unlocked and it creaked and whined open at her touch.

But one look and she knew the blood was real, and that this time there would be no reprieve.

* * * * *

Silhouette® Romantic Suspense
keeps getting hotter!
Turn the page for a sneak preview of
Wendy Rosnau's latest SPY GAMES *title*
SLEEPING WITH DANGER
Available November 2007

Silhouette® Romantic Suspense—
Sparked by Danger, Fueled by Passion!

Melita had been expecting a chaste quick kiss of the generic variety. But this kiss with Sully was the kind that sparked a dying flame to life. The kind of kiss you can't plan for. The kind of kiss memories are built on.

The memory of her murdered lover, Nemo, came to her then and she made a starved little noise in the back of her throat. She raised her arms and threaded her fingers through Sully's hair, pulled him closer. Felt his body settle, then melt into her.

In that instant her hunger for him grew, and his for her. She pressed herself to him with more urgency, and he responded in kind.

Melita came out of her kiss-induced memory of Nemo with a start. "Wait a minute." She pushed Sully away from her. "You bastard!"

She spit two nasty words at him in Greek, then wiped his kiss from her lips.

"I thought you deserved some solid proof that I'm still in one piece." He started for the door. "The clock's ticking, honey. Come on, let's get out of here."

"That's it? You sucker me into kissing you, and that's all you have to say?"

"I'm sorry. How's that?"

He didn't sound sorry in the least. "You're—"

"Getting out of this godforsaken prison cell. Stop whining and let's go."

"Not if I was being shot at sunrise. Go. You deserve whatever you get if you walk out that door."

He turned back. "Freedom is what I'm going to get."

"A second of freedom before the guards

in the hall shoot you." She jammed her hands on her hips. "And to think I was worried about you."

"If you're staying behind, it's no skin off my ass."

"Wait! What about our deal?"

"You just said you're not coming. Make up your mind."

"Have you forgotten we need a boat?"

"How could I? You keep harping on it."

"I'm not going without a boat. And those guards out there aren't going to just let you walk out of here. You need me and we need a plan."

"I already have a plan. I'm getting out of here. That's the plan."

"I should have realized that you never intended to take me with you from the very beginning. You're a liar and a coward."

Of everything she had read, there was nothing in Sully Paxton's file that hinted he was a coward, but it was the one word that seemed to register in that one-track mind of his. The look he nailed her with a second later was pure venom.

He came at her so quickly she didn't have

time to get out of his way. "You know I'm not a coward."

"Prove it. Give me until dawn. I need one more night to put everything in place before we leave the island."

"You're asking me to stay in this cell one more night...and trust you?"

"Yes."

He snorted. "Yesterday you knew they were planning to harm me, but instead of doing something about it you went to bed and never gave me a second thought. Suppose tonight you do the same? By tomorrow I might damn well be in my grave."

"Okay, I screwed up. I won't do it again." Melita sucked in a ragged breath. "I can't leave this minute. Dawn, Sully. Wait until dawn." When he looked as if he was about to say no, she pleaded, "Please wait for me."

"You're asking a lot. The door's open now. I would be a fool to hang around here and trust that you'll be back."

"What you can trust is that I want off this island as badly as you do, and you're my only hope."

"I must be crazy."

"Is that a yes?"

"Dammit!" He turned his back on her. Swore twice more.

"You won't be sorry."

He turned around. "I already am. How about we seal this new deal?"

He was staring at her lips. Suddenly Melita knew what he expected. "We already sealed it."

"One more. You enjoyed it. Admit it."

"I enjoyed it because I was kissing someone else."

He laughed. "That's a good one."

"It's true. It might have been your lips, but it wasn't you I was kissing."

"If that's your excuse for wanting to kiss me, then—"

"I was kissing Nemo."

"What's a nemo?"

Melita gave Sully a look that clearly told him that he was trespassing on sacred ground. She was about to enforce it with a warning when a voice in the hall jerked them both to attention.

She bolted away from the wall. "Get back in bed. Hurry. I'll be here before dawn."

She didn't reach the door before he snagged her arm, pulled her up against him and planted a kiss on her lips that took her completely by surprise.

When he released her, he said, "If you're confused about who just kissed you, the name's Sully. I'll be here waiting at dawn. Don't be late."

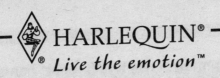

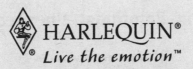

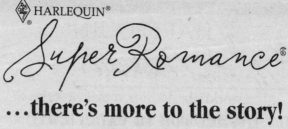
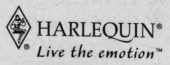

HARLEQUIN®
Presents®

The world's bestselling romance series...
The series that brings you your favorite authors,
month after month:

Helen Bianchin...Emma Darcy
Lynne Graham...Penny Jordan
Miranda Lee...Sandra Marton
Anne Mather...Carole Mortimer
Susan Napier...Michelle Reid

and many more uniquely talented authors!

Wealthy, powerful, gorgeous men...
Women who have feelings just like your own...
The stories you love, set in exotic, glamorous locations...

HARLEQUIN®
Presents®

Seduction and Passion Guaranteed!

Harlequin® Historical
Historical Romantic Adventure!

Imagine a time of chivalrous knights and unconventional ladies, roguish rakes and impetuous heiresses, rugged cowboys and spirited frontierswomen— these rich and vivid tales will capture your imagination!

Harlequin Historical... they're too good to miss!

www.eHarlequin.com

HHDIR06